Keepers & Killers

Donna Augustine

ISBN: 061585088X
ISBN-13: 978-0615850887
Strong Hold Publishing

CONTENTS

To Kel…

Edited by Express Editing Solutions

http://www.expresseditingsolutions.co.uk/

CHAPTER ONE

I was dealt pocket aces, an odd turn of luck considering how things had been going. I looked up and eyed the rest of the poker table at The Lacard Casino. I used to cocktail waitress in this very spot not long ago - the High rollers pit - where there were three types of players : the rich, the degenerate and the pro. While I stacked and restacked the chips in front of me, I sized up the other six people sitting at the table. Four rich and two degenerates, not a pro in sight; I could take down a nice pot with this hand if I played it cool.

A tingling in my skin made me turn around. I nearly jumped out of my seat when I discovered someone was standing there, lurking. It didn't help that he looked like the Russian boxer from Rocky IV. Luckily, I knew this man, and he hadn't tried to shoot me in at least a couple of months. When he had shot me, it had been on Cormac's orders, our boss. Like I've mentioned, things have been a little rough of late.

"What's up Buzz?" I asked, more interested in what the older guy in the sunglasses was doing. Did he just rub his hand because it itched or because he had good cards and he was nervous?

"Need you for another shift." His words were stilted as he spoke, probably knowing what my reaction to them would be.

"I just finished less than twenty minutes ago." I turned back toward the table, and tried to ignore his presence. The old guy just did it again. Maybe he was setting up to bluff. I hadn't been here long enough to get a read on him. It was hard to concentrate with the breathing mountain casting a shadow over me, God he was a loud breather. I wouldn't look at him, still hoping he'd leave.

"Kever's sick," he said, now with a slight whine to his tone.

I wanted to remind him that we, Alchemists that is, didn't get sick like regular people, but I couldn't say that. I had a whole table of human witnesses listening. It wouldn't matter, anyway. Kever was the king of calling out. There'd be some stupid reason his lazy butt couldn't get there. I ran my hand through my blond hair in frustration, losing a couple of strands to the cause. "Fine, but let me finish this round out."

I must have sounded a tad too eager, because just like that, all the other players at the table started to fold, even the old guy. He had been bluffing. "Forget it. I'm coming now." I threw my cards face down on the felt and stood up.

I pulled down my skirt as I stretched out my legs. I liked to show a little skin when I played, it threw some of the guys off their game. I sighed at the waste of my outfit as I headed back across the crowded casino floor, through the jingle of slot machines with their siren's song of booty to be had, toward the private elevator that would take me back to work.

It was a strange name to call what I was doing. If someone had told me a year ago that I would be operating a wormhole, I would have told them they had rocks in their head. I also would have conjured up an image of something glamorous and on the cutting edge of the latest science. Good thing I'm not a betting girl. It isn't very glamorous at all.

Wait, strike that, I am a betting girl. Working in a casino, even if it's in the super secret basement, sort of allows gambling to get under your skin. In fact, I won a few hundred off a whale playing Texas Hold'em yesterday. A whale is what we call the newbs that come to Vegas for the weekend and think they can hold their own. It's like taking candy from a baby. Normally I'd feel bad, but if they are staying here at The Lacard, they can afford the loss.

I didn't really need the money either, since I get paid a pretty penny from Cormac to work my skills keeping this wormhole operating, but I'm saving up so that if I do decide to get out of this place, I can fall of the face of the Earth. I'm thinking of buying a Caribbean island somewhere. I'll have to if I want to get far enough away from Cormac to not be found. He's got some weird way of finding me wherever I go. I can't figure out how he does it, but it's a real downer.

He's an Alchemist too, part of a group called The Keepers. I'm part alchemist on my paternal side, but I'm not one of them. If this were McDonald's, I'd be the fry girl and he'd own the chain. I just do what I have to do to get by. After all the stuff that has happened recently, I figure hanging out here might not be the worst idea - for a while, anyway.

And back to the Alchemist thing; most people think of a chemist, or would if I could tell them. We aren't, and haven't been for a long time. As for what Alchemists really are? I'm half Alchemist and still don't have it completely worked out. The main gist of it is that our brains work in strange ways that make us heal quickly and I can alter physics with my mind. All I cared about was that my feet ached, and I wished it wasn't a huge secret because I could have used a union rep. I'd barely gotten a twenty minute break before I was called back to work a double. I'd gotten better shifts when I'd been a cocktail waitress.

I took the elevator down into the lowest depths of the basement, had my eyeball scanned, and walked the long hallway that stretched out too far ahead to see to the room we used to open the wormhole. I thought to myself, as I passed by other Keepers in the cinder block and cement walkway, how amazing it was that the oddest things can become normal if you are exposed to them enough. If I had a reflector vest and a flag, you could've put me on street construction traffic, for all this fazed me. Yes, I was directing aliens, known as Fae and Werewolves to most civilians, in and out of different universes as opposed to cars, but it still felt old hat.

I opened the steel door and looked around the portal room which was some two hundred feet below the ground and had a security system that would make the CIA envious. A row of computers lined one wall, and ebony stones towered on the side where I'd open the portal. I was flying solo tonight except for the occasional Keeper poking his head in to see the half-breed phenomenon at work. Some Keepers needed a little help getting the portal going, but not me. I think that's another reason they liked me on. Everybody else got the night off when I was running things. The ebony monoliths in the room helped, but I wasn't sure exactly how.

I hopped up onto a table and crossed my legs, admiring my new sexy boots that had also gone to waste. There would always be tomorrow. I pushed my aggravation aside and reached inward, to the special spot inside of me that let me alter the physical universe, and started opening the portal. I watched the space where the wormhole would start to open glitter as the air in the room charged. The lavender sky soon peeked through the other end as I made the walls of the wormhole larger and larger, but I had to be careful. I occasionally gave it a bit too much juice and expanded it right into the walls of the room. In an area almost as large as a high school gymnasium, it was serious overkill. I didn't feel like hearing from Cormac about how he had to get the engineers back in and…blah blah blah. I told him I'd pay for it if I did it again, even though it wasn't the money that annoyed him, but the inconvenience. Have you priced out an island lately? They're pretty expensive. I really didn't want to pay for repairs, so no more fun on that scale.

There I was, sitting with this tunnel open, just

gazing at its sparkling walls and the gigantic moon at the other end. No one was there waiting on the other side; no Fae, no wolves.

So, I waited. They were probably running behind schedule. I'm not sure what time zone it was over there.

I filed my nails, looked at the funny lead walls and waited some more.

Searched the internet on my phone, held the portal open and waited. I'm really good at multitasking.

Five hours later, leaned against the wall, phone dead with no charger, I heard the door open.

"Jo, Cormac said they bailed. You can shut it down," Dodd said.

I turned to look at where Dodd stood at the door to the portal room. Dodd is Cormac's right hand. He's okay. He was dark haired, good looking and used it to its very fullest advantage. The staff of The Lacard often joked that the only reason anyone ever got fired or hired around here was to supply Dodd with variety. I didn't care how many girls he slept with. The only thing that bugged me was he had been there the night I'd been shot and hadn't done a damn thing to help. That really sticks in my craw.

"I've been holding this thing open for five hours. Five!" I held my hand up with my fingers outspread, just in case he was a little slow on math today. "He just realized it now?"

"Sorry, kid," he said, but his face didn't look very sorry and the crinkling at his eyes portrayed an altogether different emotion.

"Sorry, yeah, you guys are good at throwing that word around." He knew exactly what I meant and the bastard smirked, giving up on any ruse of regret. "It's still not funny. You're lucky I didn't scar." My hand instinctively ran over the spot on my scalp where the bullets had entered and been pushed back out by my body.

I collapsed the wormhole quickly. Even though I had been a slow starter, I was the strongest operator they had. Ever since I blew up the mountain, a couple of months ago, I'd been able to open and close them easily. It didn't used to be like that. I used to suck. I still suck at a lot of other Alchemy things, like turning base metal into gold. I was hoping like hell I'd gotten the eternal youth thing worked out. Yes, I'm young and pretty, and I want to stay that way. But with the way our brains worked, you didn't really know for sure until you got old or didn't. Our subconscious has lots of control over how things work in our bodies and is really good at circumventing the normal human downfalls, but it is like being in a marriage where the two spouses didn't speak. I don't know what is for dinner until it is hot and in front of me. And that's if I am lucky. Some full blooded Alchemists age, and don't get any of the perks other than a claim to the blood line. Big whoop! You can't tell anyone about it anyway.

"Cormac wants to know if you're staying here at the casino," he asked.

I gathered up my phone and purse from the room then turned back to him quick enough to catch his eyes on my butt.

"You can stop staring at my butt, and you can tell Cormac, that like every other night this past week, I will be going home to my trailer." I had initially been staying in the extra room in Cormac's penthouse but I felt I needed a sense of autonomy before his massive ego tried to run amok all over the independence I had left. His personality could bulldoze its way over most people and I refused to fall victim.

"You know what a pain in the ass this is for me?" he asked, as if I were unaware of Cormac's controlling nature.

"Sorry," I said with a visible smirk. See how he liked it.

He rolled his eyes as he held the door for me.

"A car is waiting out the main entrance. Cormac said that none of the bus drivers will stop for you anymore, so unless you want to walk?" He told my back as I walked down the hall.

I spun around and opened my mouth to speak but Dodd beat me to it.

"Really Jo? I know you're stubborn, but that's just stupid."

I was too exhausted to argue, and the person I really wanted to argue with wasn't there. I turned, without another word, and made my way back upstairs to the grand entrance on the strip. I relented and took the car to my trailer.

What an odd sight it made as I got out of a midnight black stretch limo. I'd never been embarrassed about being poor, but I was strangely awkward about showing up in a nice car? God, I had more issues than I even realized.

I climbed from the car before the driver could open the door, somehow thinking that would make it better. The driver got out anyway and tried to insist on escorting me to my door but I told him it wasn't safe for him, slipped him a twenty and told him to get lost. I could tell he was about to start arguing but then someone screamed, "Hey, look, fresh meat!" from a couple of trailers over and he ran back to the safety of the car and sped away.

I felt all eyes on me; nothing direct of course - I'd tussled with a couple of the people here and no one had the balls to take me on anymore - just some peripheral views and curious gaps in mini blinds. When are people going to realize that you can still see them looking through the gap?

I'd made it ten steps before my awkwardness turned into irritation. "I'm a high class hooker! Are you all happy?" And just like that, everyone went back to their business. We had a few resident hookers, so my outburst satisfied their curiosity. All was right in their world again, mystery solved.

It was probably stupid to have qualified myself as a high class hooker. What? Am I too good for the street corner variety? I mean, if I'm going to pretend I'm a hooker, I probably shouldn't put on airs.

I stopped thinking about it once I saw my oasis. No one else would look at my old run down trailer, with rusted spots on the paneling, and think 'oasis,' but to me it was a little chunk of peace in a chaotic world. After working for twenty hours straight at Micky C's, as I liked to call The Lacard, my bed was the only thing on my mind. A fleeting thought of what an ass Cormac was to put me on so many hours straight fluttered through my brain, right before sleep chased it away.

Some unknown time later, I squinted my eyes open. It was still dark. That surprised me, since I thought I'd be out for at least a solid ten. My stupid electronic clock was down to two digits left, one of which was the second hour, which read two. It couldn't be two in the afternoon because it was still dark. Could I have slept a full day away? I'd been exhausted. Running a wormhole always does that to me. I think it's the radiation we absorb in the process. Radiation isn't a big deal to us in certain doses, but it would fry our commuters if we didn't absorb it and shield them.

Then it hit me. Why was there no noise? In my particular trailer park, two in the afternoon was dead quiet; midnight, on the other hand, was a rip roaring good time for all. What the hell was going on out there? I stumbled from the bed, alarmed, and threw on the first sort of clean pair of jeans I could find before heading outside.

Cement and cars. Rows and rows of expensive looking cars in every color of the rainbow greeted me. Gone was my blue sky and desert air. I had cement, more cars than any sane person needed and central air? Who air conditions their garage?

"I'm going to kill him," I said as I slipped on the flip flops I had left by the door.

Dodd, with the worst timing of anyone I knew, had the misfortune of being the first one I laid my eyes on. He was wearing a tank top and jeans looking like he was part of a construction crew and while he was directing several of Cormac's guys into the garage with potted plants. "Oh hey! You're up," he greeted me in a jovial manner.

"Where is he?" I asked, focused on the only thing I cared about at that moment.

"Do you like it? Since it's Cormac's garage, it's really private. We thought you might like some shrubs to warm up the place," he said as he directed the guys to place a bush on either side of the doorway I stood in.

"Remove the bushes," I told the guys that had just placed them down. Unlike Dodd, they picked up quickly on my mood. They took their bushes and stepped back away from me.

"That's not nice, Jo. Don't scare the gardeners. They're just trying to make the place cozy for you," Dodd chided.

"Warm up all the cement? They're going to die in here. It's an indoor garage!" Even as I said it, I wondered why I bothered. Let their plants die. I stormed out of the garage as he tried to explain that they were going to rotate them in and out and wasn't that just the most brilliant idea.

It took me all of five minutes to make it to the top floor penthouse Cormac lived in. It didn't matter to me one bit if he wasn't there. I'd sit and wait. He'd have to come back at some point.

When the elevator doors slid open, Sumo wrestlers were standing guard like they sometimes did; but that didn't mean anything. Their work habits had no rhyme or reason to me. I was starting to get the impression that they showed up when they felt like working and really served no purpose other than to look menacing. Anyone that had met Cormac in person wouldn't mess with him, well except for me. He could be one really scary guy. If I had a little more sense and a little less balls, I wouldn't mess with him either, but life makes you who you are and I don't see much of a reason to fight my nature.

People spend their lives in therapy to fight their natural inclinations. Day in and day out, not doing what they desire in the hopes of being this better, happier and more successful person. It just seems like an awful lot of work to do something that doesn't come naturally. I'm not saying therapy is bad, it's just too much work for me. I'm more about embracing my broken self for all that she can be. And that included the girl who was about to have a smack down with her boss, who could kick her ass all the way down the Vegas Strip. Ugh, when had I started calling him my boss? It felt like it snuck up on me out of nowhere. I had to break that bad habit real quick.

I stormed down his hallway; the various priceless paintings did nothing for my mood today, as I stared at the carved wooden door to his place. The handle was locked and I pounded on the door like a raving lunatic. I'd show him who's boss. I should have kept my key, instead of making some symbolic show of declaring my independence and leaving it in the middle of the table with a big note saying I didn't need it, on the day I'd moved out.

He took his time answering the door so Ben must not have been around. He was another one of Cormac's quasi-servants. Ben was a lanky guy that liked to masquerade as a door man. He pissed me off too. He did anything Cormac wanted. They all did. That was enough to piss me off, stupid puppets.

"Jo, I've been expecting you," he said when he opened the door.

Whether I wanted to or not, I always got a little flustered when I saw Cormac. The term 'tall, dark and handsome' probably originated with him, way back when he was born, whenever that might have been. He looked thirtyish but when his pale blue eyes roved over you, it felt as if he were ancient. They were intense. And when he did it like he was now, a slow, roving appraisal, I always felt a tingle shoot through me. I tried to swallow back the lump in my throat and speak.

"Cormac, I…"

"Lacey is here."

My words died as I watched him walk, dressed in his standard black slacks and white shirt that contrasted starkly to his tan skin and black hair, into his beige living room. He liked everything around him to be beige. I didn't really get it. He was the least beige person I have ever met. I wondered if he thought hiding in his beige penthouse and wearing expensive clothing made who he really was less obvious. Someone should clue him in; it was like a panther stalking his prey in a snow field.

I walked in behind him, already annoyed. Cormac had formed some sort of indefinable relationship with Lacey, who was also my best friend. Actually, she was my *only* friend, which is what elevated her status to 'best.' If you only had one donut, wouldn't it be the best donut there ever was?

"Hi Jo! Cormac said you might drop by. Want a glass of wine?" she offered from her seat on the couch. She must of spent hours fixing her bleached blond hair to get it that perfectly straight and smooth. Her little blue dress rode up just high enough to show off enough firm thigh without looking too slutty and, unless she'd gotten some work done without telling me, she had doubled up on the push up bras. I watched Cormac settle down on the other side of the couch as she smiled from ear to ear, her red lipstick showing off her super white teeth.

Cormac had planned this well. I pretended my eyeballs had weights on them to stop myself from rolling them to the back of my head. Every time he pissed me off lately, Lacey wouldn't be far from his side.

Instead of staring at the two of them, I'd rather stare out at the beautiful expanse of Vegas that was displayed by the wall of glass. But I couldn't, I didn't want him to know I might miss this place, even a little.

They were ridiculous. The girl that played every man she knew was sitting there waiting for crumbs of attention. She said they were friends, but I could see in her big Bambi eyes how badly she wanted more. She might not if she knew everything I knew, but I hadn't told her. It was something that plagued me daily. She had no idea who he was, or how ruthless he could be. She didn't know the casino was a front, used simply to disguise the energy pouring out of the wormhole in the basement. I couldn't tell her any of it. I'd signed a contract that might have some crazy ramifications if I did.

She also didn't know how close and personal I'd been with Cormac. She was my donut, she wouldn't go near him if she knew. I hadn't told her that either, even though I could. I don't know why. I just hadn't. I tried to not think about it because it made me feel things that I didn't like or want.

"Why is my trailer in your garage?" I asked calmly; I refused to drop the subject simply because Lacey was there. This had nothing to do with secret stuff. He wasn't going to manipulate this situation on me, not again.

"Oh that! Isn't that nice? I mentioned to Cormac how you always leave the casino so late after you're done in the counting room. I didn't think it was safe, so he came up with that. Wasn't it sweet?" She smiled again and sipped her wine. Lacey thought I was counting money in the basement since I wasn't good with customers. Confirming I sucked with people was a lot easier than telling her I could alter physics with my brain.

I stood, legs spread apart and arms crossed, staring at them. "You did that for her?" I raised my eyebrows, daring him to lie to me.

Lacey, so buried in the vision of what she wanted him to be, missed my sarcasm and simply smiled at him with an adoring look upon her face. I wanted to drag her off the couch and scream some sense into her.

"I listen to her," he said as he leaned back on the couch.

"Did you do this for her, Cormac? Is that what you are saying?" I took a step forward as I pointed in his direction.

"I didn't want her to worry," he non-answered. His stare was intent and his voice a little softer when he continued. "I heard they were doing some rearranging at your development. I'd hate to see things floating all around and unsettled. This place is more secure for you." He put his feet up on the cocktail table and crossed his ankles.

"I want it moved back. Today." I punctuated the word today as I stabbed the air with my finger.

He said nothing, just stared at me at first. Seconds ticked by and I thought I he wasn't even going to give me a response, but then, he quirked an eyebrow and crossed his arms over his chest.

I couldn't even think of a word that would satisfy the anger I felt for him right then and there.

"Jo, why are you being so rude to him? He did you a favor. Your development was a dump," Lacey said in his defense as she set her wine glass down in front of her.

I turned back toward her. "Because it's not his call."

"Fine. Cormac, maybe you should put it back if she doesn't appreciate it." Her body language added *if she's going to be ungrateful,* as she leaned back against the couch.

I watched him. He didn't even turn and acknowledge that she had spoken, just continued to stare at me as I stared back.

And then he said only one word, "No." He didn't yell, simply shrugged his shoulders in a nonchalant manner. He'd just drawn a line in the sand. Worse, he'd practically dared me to cross it. I had to decide if I would.

I toed the line in my imagination but then I looked at Lacey. She'd sensed something too, even through that thick coat of adoration. Her body language stiffened a bit as she got a hint that the man next to her wasn't a kitten but a lion. I knew what the ramifications of her knowing would be; another reason I wanted her as far from him as possible. I could handle this, she couldn't. I should have gotten us both out of here months ago, but back then, I had been more alarmed and concerned by what was going on around me than what was happening right next to me.

At the time, I'd just discovered two things about a man I thought I'd killed. Firstly, he was alive, and secondly, he was a U.S. senator, and a powerful one at that. I'd already known the third thing: he was dangerous. What made him dangerous? He wasn't human, that was for sure. Anything that could make it out of a collapsing wormhole and not be crushed was bad news. He also hated me. I wasn't sure why. I hadn't thought to ask before I kicked his butt.

"Why do you keep playing with that nickel?" Lacey asked.

I looked down at my hand. I hadn't even realized I'd pulled the nickel I always carried out of my pocket. I felt the cool metal in my hand and tested its hardness with my finger. Nope, still nickel. I could open a huge wormhole but I couldn't do the simplest of the Alchemist tricks. Having a pile of gold would make life much simpler in the future.

"It's lucky," I said to try and explain this weird habit I'd adopted.

"Why's that?" Cormac asked, as his eyes silently mocked.

"Cormac, I swear you just like to rile her up," Lacey told him and as she playfully swatted at him.

I shook my head. I couldn't watch this for one more second. "I'll see you later." I mentally backed away from the line as I physically left the room.

He'd played that hand well, knowing I wouldn't drag out this fight in front of Lacey. I wouldn't pull her any deeper into this gunfight. She couldn't take the bullets.

CHAPTER TWO

"I know you're there. You might as well walk with me," I yelled back to Buzz, who was following me and not very well. The guy was so bad at tailing I couldn't figure out if I was supposed to know he was there or if Cormac was delusional about his abilities. He'd tripped on the stairs chasing me out of the casino front doors, for Heaven's sake.

"It's not my fault. He told me to follow you," Buzz said.

If Dodd was Cormac's right hand, Buzz was his left, and Cormac was right handed.

"Where are we going?" he asked as he fell into step beside me.

I looked up at the big blond. "I'll deal with you coming but you're on a need to know basis."

"Shit. That means I'm not gonna like it." I saw a bead of sweat on his forehead. "What do I need to know?"

"Nothing," I replied as I kept to my brisk pace.

He silently kept step alongside me as we dodged between people on the busy Vegas Strip.

"Can't we ever take a car?" I watched him eye up one of the many passing taxis longingly.

"I like the exercise." It was true, even in the heat. I liked the feel of my muscles pumping and my body moving. All I needed right now was an iPod loaded up with some Imagine Dragons and My Chemical Romance. Too bad I was afraid to close off my hearing these days. I wanted to be alert to everything.

"But you don't need any."

I knew I was thin and I took that to be his meaning. "Everybody should get exercise. You do."

"No, I never exercise. Hate the stuff," he said, emphasizing the word hate.

"Then how are you so muscular..." My words died as realization hit me. My entire life, I'd always eaten as much as I'd wanted but I had always burned it off running. Well, I've still been eating like a pig but haven't been running at all. I'd also not gained a pound. "You're right. How does that work exactly?"

"No clue. Ask Cormac."

"I can't. I'm not speaking to him until my trailer is back where it's supposed to be. I've been living in his garage for two days and I don't like it." We crossed another street, nearing our destination.

Buzz let out a deep belly laugh in response.

"Why is that funny?"

"Cause he's never gonna move it back," He said and continued to laugh loudly. A few people stared at him as we walked past thanks to his loud guffaws.

"And that's funny?" I asked, getting a little more irritated with each second.

"Yeah…isn't it?" He wiped a tear from his eye.

I threw him a frosty glare as I sat on a bench across the street from the Paris Casino.

"Now what are we doing?"

"Waiting." My desire to enlighten him was even less so than before.

"For what?"

"Them." I tilted my head in the direction of the crowd. I watched as the large, blond, Viking throwback ogled the crowd.

I pulled out sunglasses and a baseball cap, shoving my long blond hair through the hole in the back of the cap, and opened a newspaper. I watched over the top of the page as the people poured in and out of the casino.

"If you are staying, can you try to be a bit less conspicuous? I'm not sitting here actually *reading* the paper." I shook it out as I emphasized my point.

He sat down and crowded the small bench. "Sports?" He held his hand out to me as he waited.

I handed him his requested section and he fell quiet for all of five minutes. "Why do we care about these people?"

"I can't tell you. You'll spill the beans to Cormac," I told him as I scanned the travel section. Which part of the Caribbean was best…hmmm, decisions, decisions.

"I won't." His voice sounded slightly hurt.

I turned my head toward him and raised my eyebrows. "Really? I tell you and that's the end of it?" He at least had the courtesy to blush when I called him out on his lie. Why I felt bad about hurting his feelings was beyond me.

"Maybe I've reported on you in the past, but I won't this time if you tell me." There was hope in his voice. I hated squashing hope.

"You go running and blathering to him, I swear, every time you tail me we'll be shopping." I used my sternest schoolmarm voice.

He visibly swallowed, remembering the two weeks he followed me around the mall. "That really sucked."

"There's a town hall going on in one of the venue rooms in there." I looked back at the Paris Casino again, the crowds still filing in, and wondered if there was a back entrance he had used or if he'd already been inside when we'd gotten there.

"What's that?"

"It's basically when a politician holds court." There were Secret Service stationed by the doors; he must be in there.

"And why would...Oh no, we gotta go. We gotta go *now*!" Buzz stood and grabbed my arm, pulling me with him. "Cormac doesn't like this guy and I was specifically told to not let you go near him!"

I pulled at my arm, still firmly in his grasp. "I'm not going anywhere and if you try to drag me, I'll scream so loud, everyone within five miles will wonder how you're torturing the sweet little blond girl." I accented my words with the sweetest innocent smile I could fake.

"Cormac…" his words died abruptly.

"Cormac what?" I pulled at my arm again, stuck in his beefy unyielding grip.

"Caitlin?" A male voice yelled from a short distance away. His voice rang in my head and nipped at my memories. "Caitlin! Oh my god, it is you!" his voice was as shocked as I felt.

I turned to see Rick's face and I was speechless; sweet Rick who had shared a foster home with me. The same Rick who had given me a Monet book I had duct taped together and still have to this day. My childhood protector, alive and well, and fully grown. I hadn't seen him since he was a teenager, but even then, he'd been something special.

"Is this guy bothering you?" He eyed Buzz warily as he stood next to me.

"No, he's a friend," I said, once I finally found my voice. I pulled my arm from Buzz's now loose grip.

"Yes, I'm *Caitlin's* friend," Buzz said.

"You look fantastic!" he exclaimed as he looked me up and down.

"So do you." And he did look good. He had the same tawny hair and warm chocolate eyes, kind eyes. My child's heart recognized the boy in the man. I remembered looking into those eyes and feeling just slightly less alone in the world.

"I really want to catch up with you but I'm working right now. If I don't get inside in the next couple of minutes my boss will have my head! Here, take my card and please call me." I took the card and he embraced me suddenly.

"I will," I said as I hugged him back, not

remembering the last person I'd hugged.

He left and I watched him walk briskly into the Paris Casino and my mouth grew dry as foreboding filled me. I looked down at the card. Rick Tabarnink, Aid to Senator Core.

"*Caitlin.* And I don't have to keep that a secret because you didn't tell it to me." He gloated and all my feelings of guilt disappeared.

"Buzz, you're really pissing me off today. I swear, keep it up and I'm going to need some new shoes." I walked away from him, leaving my observation post. If a man I hadn't seen since my teens spotted me, I needed to find a better place to perch, because my disguise wasn't cutting it. I couldn't take the chance that Rick would draw attention to me if I was in the same place when they came out.

"Yeah, Boss?" Buzz answered his phone as I scoped out a good hidey hole that could fit him as well as myself.

"Gotcha." He shoved his phone in his pocket and looked at me. "Cormac wants us back."

"You head back. I'm busy," I told him as I eyed up smaller spots. If he was leaving, finding a spot would be easier.

"Jo, the boss wants you back. Please don't make this hard on me," he pleaded.

"We are standing in the middle of the Vegas Strip. You can't man handle me back there without drawing one hell of a crowd. I'm doing my thing. Deal with it and go handle yours."

Then I made the mistake of turning my back on him.

"Just remember this wasn't my choice," he said.

I turned, a bad feeling forming with those words, just in time to see him hit me over the head. My vision went fuzzy, then black.

CHAPTER THREE

"What did you think you were doing?" Cormac's voice pierced my brain.

I was just coming to. How did he know I was even awake yet?

"I can't believe that bastard whacked me on the back of the head. That's just wrong." I felt along my scalp but couldn't find the bump that rightfully should've been there.

"He knows how to follow orders." I loved the deep timbre of Cormac's voice, even when what he said pissed me off.

I felt a bed underneath me and, even though I wasn't ready to look at him, I opened my eyes to see where the hell I was. My trailer? That was a bit unexpected. And there, at the foot of the bed, loomed Cormac, one foot resting on the frame of the bed as he bent over slightly, leaning his crossed arms on it. His crisp white shirt sleeves were rolled up, as always. I couldn't decide if he didn't button them to show off his muscular arms or because he hated the confinement of civilized clothing. Not that he came off as ill mannered, but there was something just beneath the surface that pricked at my senses in the most disconcerting way and whispered of baser origins.

"Aren't all of you people really old? That's what Tracker told me. So, are you like chivalrous type old? Or are you club a girl over the head kinda old?" I watched his stone expression, which didn't crack a bit. "Because between the shooting and now the hitting, I'm starting to harbor some suspicions about what era you people really come from. Chemists, my ass."

His face was still stone.

"Get up, Caitlin. I want to talk." He pushed off the bed and straightened to his full height.

"First off, don't call me that. My name is Jo, and I'm not going to be civil to you until this trailer is back in its proper location." I threw my arm across my eyes as I lay there, knowing it was futile. These guys never took the hint. "I don't know which is worse, that you had me shot or that you moved my trailer. You know what, Cormac? You need to learn boundaries."

"I don't believe in boundaries." I heard him rustling around my room but still wouldn't look at him. "I'm not leaving 'til we talk. I'll be in that little box you call a living room, waiting for you." I heard his footsteps retreat.

I sat up. If talking to Cormac meant him leaving me alone right now, I'd get up. I walked in and found him riffling through my fridge.

"Don't you keep any food in this hovel?" He asked as he moved on to my limited cabinets.

"No," I said. "What time is it?" I asked. I didn't have a clock in the living room.

"One thirty" he said as he glanced down at a platinum watch.

I held up my finger, and motioned for him to give me a minute as I paused by the front door. Thirty seconds later, the rap came. I didn't need to ask who it was, I just opened it.

"Good afternoon, Miss Jo." A man in a Lacard uniform came in carrying a tray.

"Hello Alex," I greeted him. I'd had the same waiter every day.

"Oh, hello, Sir! Was there to be something additional today? I didn't see it on the schedule." He fumbled into his pocket with his free hand and pulled out his pad to locate the details.

"No, just the usual," I answered to save him the trouble.

He smiled, relieved to not have forgotten the owner's food. "Would you like it in your regular spot?" he asked.

"That would be wonderful," I said as I stepped out of his way to allow him access to the spot in front of the sofa.

It took him a few moments to arrange everything as he carried in a table and set it up. He covered it in a white cloth and set down the silver service.

As he finished up and was about to leave, I hit Cormac in the arm. "Give me a twenty. I don't have cash ready for him. I *overslept*," I said, as I laid the sarcasm on liberally.

He pulled a wad of cash, held by a gold money clip, out of his black pants. "I've only got hundreds," he said, fingering through the bills.

"That's fine," I said, as I took the first bill off of his bank roll.

I handed Alex the bill. He smiled and told me he'd be back in an hour to clean up as he left.

"You are getting room service out here?" Cormac asked once the door shut. He walked over and lifted the lid to see what food I had.

"I am technically in the casino, aren't I?" I watched him place the lid back over the dish as he walked back to the kitchenette.

He let out a deep laugh. "Got any anything to drink other than this jug of wine?" He leaned down and looked in the lower cabinet.

"That's pre-move. The good stuff is behind the paper towels, top right. You have quite a wine cellar here."

"Any scotch?"

"No. None of my guests drink that."

"Are you always going to be so prickly?"

"Must be the company." I sat on the couch and pulled my legs up underneath me, watching his large frame move around my tiny home, completely out of place. His clothing probably cost more than my entire trailer, with the exception of the Monet painting.

"What did you want to talk about?" I asked, eager to get the discussion over with and him out of my haven.

He moved out of the kitchen area, empty

handed. For the first time, I realized how small my living room was. "If we were on speaking terms, I would've informed you that I don't want you going anywhere near Senator Core. I've already got him under surveillance."

"And we know how well your surveillance works," I said as I reminded him of another time his men had lost Tracker, the Wolf who had started the problem with the wormholes and tried to shut down The Lacard portal. He'd also had some unknown connection to the senator. I'd inadvertently killed Tracker in the mountain collapse.

"I'm meeting with Vitor tonight," he continued, as he ignored my jab. "Would you like to be there?"

Once Vitor had been cleared of any participation in interfering with the wormholes, he and Cormac had formed a tentative truce again. No one on this side of the hole, as we liked to call it, had actually seen Vitor. All correspondence had gone through messengers. But a subject like the senator was too sensitive to discuss through messaging.

Did I want to be there? Hell yes! He knew it, too. So what was the price?

"Yes, there's a catch," he answered before I asked.

"Which is?"

"You're smart and tough. You're also determined to be involved; it would be much easier if we weren't at odds. I'm holding out an olive branch." He leaned his hip against my counter, crossing his ankles in a relaxed posture, like my answer wasn't that important.

"What about my trailer? I want it moved back." I countered, picking at my fries, feigning equal indifference.

"Can't do it. They've already moved another into its spot," he shrugged his shoulders.

"Which I'm sure you had nothing to do with." I waved my fry accusingly at him before I ate it.

"It's done. Does it matter?"

It did, but I wanted to hear what info Vitor would have, so I simply nodded. "Fine. Truce. What time?"

"I'll come get you at eleven tonight."

I stood to get up and his large body followed me into the paneled hallway. My hallway barely accommodated me, so to say it was a tight squeeze was an understatement.

"Why are you following me? Aren't we done?" I turned and asked. I preferred the hallway to my bedroom to find out what else he wanted.

I pressed myself as close to the wall as I could and was still only a hair's breadth away from him. "No more solo trips. We are either in this together or we aren't, and trust me, you want to be on my team." It was a statement, not a question.

"Great, now back up. You're getting awfully close for a guy that has a girlfriend." I stood still, and waited for him to retreat now that he'd said his piece.

"I don't have a girlfriend," his eyes were intent on mine.

"Does Lacey know that? Maybe you should make it clear to her, because I think that's where she's heading." His scent surrounded me and did funny things to my senses.

He leaned his forearm on the wall next to me. "There is nothing between Lacey and I. If I wanted Lacey, I would have had her, but that's none of your business."

"Hmmm, it appears you do have some boundaries after all. But, it is my business, she's my friend. If you don't want a relationship with her, then at minimum you are screwing with her emotions. That's not cool." I stared back at him and refused to give up any ground.

He came a hair closer and I could feel his body graze mine. "Since you want to get personal, if she's such a close friend, how come you never told her anything that happened with us?" he asked in a voice that was slightly deeper.

"Because nothing of importance happened." Just because it comes to mind every time I see him, that doesn't mean anything.

He placed a flat hand on the other side of my head as he leaned in. My breath held and stopped as he moved closer and then his mouth passed by mine and moved toward my ear. "You ran pretty hard from nothing." His breath sent shivers down my spine. I took a ragged breath in as he pushed off the wall and left.

CHAPTER FOUR

"Where are we going?" We'd been driving for twenty minutes, into the middle of the desert, in a two seat Ferrari. I was on Cormac proximity overload. And why was it so goddamn sexy watching a guy drive a stick shift? Didn't matter, the last thing I wanted was to be sitting there like Lacey, all doe eyed. Nope, not for me. It was probably some kind of crazy Alchemist pheromones he was throwing off, giving me a contact high.

"His estate. Would you rather have the windows down? I can turn off the air," he asked as I angled my face toward the crack in the window like a dog, searching for ,fresh air.

"No," I answered. It probably wouldn't help anyway. We'd been driving for a while in nothing but blackness. "Why all the way out here? Didn't he come through the portal in the casino? Wouldn't that have been easier?" I readjusted myself in the soft leather seat, angled away from him.

"He came over through one of the other portals. He felt more comfortable on his territory and I didn't care either way." He toyed with the radio and flipped through a quick succession of channels until he stopped on Desert Rose by Sting.

"How many other wormholes do you have going on?" I asked as the melody filled the car.

"A few. Since they've got to be spaced out, I can't manage all of them personally." He turned right off the main road. "We're here."

The driveway was the only one I'd seen for miles and it was so long it could've been mistaken for a road if it hadn't been marked as a private entrance. Lights pointed upward and lit the Willow Acacia trees that lined the drive all the way to the house.

"No gates?" I asked, thinking that this place would have state of the art security, gates at the least.

"They don't need them. I know Vitor seems civilized, but not all of his brethren are quite so refined. The Fae have other ways of keeping out unwanted guests."

We finally pulled into the circular drive. A lighted fountain spewed water in the center of the paver driveway of the sprawling ranch house with a Spanish tiled roof and stucco façade. It was massive, spreading out before us in both directions.

"This place looks fit for royalty." I looked at the lead paned windows and the ornate entrance.

"Vitor is a prince on his planet."

"Really?" I couldn't decide whether I thought that was cool or pretentious. "Is anybody going to come out?" A prince should have some sort of staff, you would think.

"No. It's not their way. To the Fae, greeting doesn't happen until you enter their domain. If one did come out, it wouldn't be in welcome. Allowing you to come to them is considered proper etiquette." He left the car sitting in the drive, walked up the steps to the front door and went to open it.

I stored that little nugget away. Fae come out... run for the hills.

I climbed the couple of stairs to the large double doors and hesitated as I watched Cormac stroll in. He paused at the open door and waited for me, his eyes telling me not to worry, he had my back. We had beef, Cormac and I, but the same thing that kept me on at the casino pushed at me now. There was a connection there that I'd never had with anyone else. Maybe it was because he knew me for what I was. There was nothing to hide with him. I'd never had that. Ever. And as long as he wasn't the one trying to kill me, I didn't think he'd let anyone else do it either. And that was a good thing? What the hell was wrong with me?

I turned my head back to eye up the distance to the car, wondering if he left the keys inside, when his hand wrapped around mine and pulled me in. "Chill out! I was coming." I hate when I feel like he is herding me. Pushy man.

I snatched my hand away as I followed him down a terra cotta tiled hallway into a great room. The entire house was decorated in a southwestern style. Glass doors overlooked a lighted pool with a waterfall set into the corner. But it was the people that my eyes came to rest on. Vitor stood off to the side, not far from the doors, looking as refined as ever. An older, aristocratic woman sat on one of the two couches that faced each other. Her grey hair was pulled into a chignon, showing off Tahitian pearls at her neck. A forty something year old man sat across from her, dressed similarly to Vitor, in khakis and a polo shirt.

"It's nice to see you, Jo," Vitor greeted me and nodded to Cormac.

To say the moment was awkward would've been like saying Smallpox had been a minor bug. I smiled over at the other people in the room, to help break the tension. You knew things were bad when I was trying to be the socially correct one.

Vitor introduced the woman on the couch as his mother, Iselda, and the gentleman as his cousin, Philip.

"Come, I'd love to show Jo the grounds a little," Vitor said. Cormac and I followed him out onto the back patio area and he shut the doors behind us. "I've heard whispers of what you want to discuss. I'd prefer to keep this private. My mother doesn't like the unrest she's been feeling in our people," Vitor explained as the three of us made our way around the pool. Lights illuminated flowerbeds in the darkness, and it took my mind back to another evening on a rooftop.

The three of us walked a bit further down a paver pathway, with me in the center. Every time either of them moved, I made sure to realign myself back in the center. It wasn't that I thought Cormac would try to have a go at Vitor, I just wasn't sure he wouldn't. Even though Vitor had been cleared of any wrongdoing, these two were far from cordial.

"Any word on Hammond?" Vitor asked.

"No," I replied. Hammond, my father, had been crushed in a cave after I had exploded a wormhole. I'd known him for less than an hour before I'd inadvertently buried him alive. He'd been working for the opposition, which made it complicated. His possible death still roiled my emotions.

"Do you have..." Vitor started to speak.

"Drop the subject," Cormac said in a peremptory tone from behind me, and cut off his words.

Vitor eyed Cormac and I could see he was weighing his actions. I didn't think he would have a chance in hell of taking on Cormac, no matter how much he'd like to. Cormac was larger but it wasn't a size thing; I didn't know what kind of fairy tricks Vitor might have, but that still didn't change my mind. It was more of a civilized, or uncivilized thing. Uncivilized might sound bad but not in a fight. Civilized was great for teas and dinner parties. If my life is on the line, I want someone who doesn't hold back. When you're staring down death, nothing's off limits.

"Vitor, do you have any idea who, or what, Core is?" I asked before this situation devolved into a wasted trip to the desert.

As soon as Vitor broke eye contact with Cormac, I knew it was back under control, at least for the moment.

"No. His human records, as I'm sure you know, have him born to a normal family from the suburbs of Vegas. Obviously he's not. I've seen him from a distance, a handful of times, but I thought he was one of Tracker's wolves initially." He spoke mostly to me.

"Couldn't you tell he wasn't a wolf?" I hadn't known but couldn't the Fae sense these things?

"No, I never got that close to him. Is he a large problem?" he asked, worry in his voice.

"He might be," Cormac answered. I guess he didn't care if Vitor considered him part of the conversation or not. "Jo had a little run in with him not long ago."

"What happened?"

I knew Vitor had a soft spot for me, but I didn't realize how much until that second; the concern I heard in those words shocked me.

"I'm handling it." Cormac started to circle around me and I moved with him, so he had to either step over me or stop. "Do you know anything or not?"

Yep, and there was Cormac pissing a circle all around me. For someone who was looking cozy with my best friend, he sure did like to mark me as his territory. I wondered if he did this with all the people that worked with him. It was starting to piss me off, pun intended.

"Vitor, we think this guy is bad news. We know he was mixed up in what went down on the mountain," I interjected, trying to bring the focus back to me.

"If he's been going back and forth from my planet, how has he been getting over here without you knowing?" Vitor asked Cormac, throwing a jibe back.

"I don't know. Maybe he had some help." Cormac left little doubt about who he thought might have helped him. I knew he didn't believe it; he was just antagonizing Vitor.

"Are you accusing me of something?" Vitor took a step closer and I thought I'd get smushed between the two of them.

"Can the two of you play nice for a couple of minutes?" I said, at about my wits' end. "I'm the only one that got close to this guy and I'm telling you, he's bad. Every cell in my body is screaming it. You guys need to get along, at least until we figure out who he is."

They both backed up slightly.

Cormac spoke first. "None of the operators recognized him coming through the portals. Either someone is lying or he had one hell of a disguise."

"I'll see what I can come up with," Vitor relented.

"When I was in the mountain with Tracker, he said that their race kept a history of all of the races. Is there any way to get access to that?"

Cormac shot me a look. I knew he was annoyed this was the first he'd heard of this. Geez, it isn't like I do it on purpose, but reporting back every single word ever said is a new thing for me and I'm not really into it.

"They don't give anyone access to anything they don't have to. Plus, after Tracker's disappearancc, neither you or Cormac are on the list of people they feel like helping out. Rumor has it that if they didn't need Keepers, they'd be picking you all off as quick as they could. Watch your back." That last little bit was said directly to me. I got the impression he'd be in front of the line to pick off Cormac if he thought it was feasible. It was becoming all to obvious that the only people Cormac played nice with were his own.

"We'll be in touch. In the meantime, keep this quiet," Cormac ordered.

"Of course," Vitor said, insulted.

Cormac pushed me to the exit and I pushed back, annoyed at his high handedness but continued out anyway. I didn't want to give these two and excuse to start tussling.

By time we got back in the car, I was exhausted. I wasn't sure if it was from worrying about who the hell the senator was or the tension of diffusing Cormac and Vitor.

"What's the deal with you two? Has it always been like this?" I asked as I leaned back in the car.

"Like what?" Cormac asked as we drove along back into the city.

"Is that a joke?" Please tell me he's kidding and that this isn't what he views as normal interaction.

He cracked a smile. "Yes. We've never clicked but he's just getting on my nerves more often lately."

About twenty minutes later we turned off the Strip down a darkened road that wasn't much more than an alleyway, sandwiched by two brick faced buildings both about four or five stories tall. The road was narrow but looked like it had been paved recently.

"Where are we?" I asked as I looked around. I

followed him out of the car. A kid of no more than eighteen, who must have been lingering in the shadows, came forward and Cormac tossed him his keys.

"We're at The Cave." He waited until I caught up to him. "Stay close to me. This place can be a bit unsavory," he said and he put a hand on the small of my back as we walked toward a solid steel door that swung open as we neared it. A strange girl with purple streaked hair stood by the door but didn't speak as she closed it after us.

"What is this place?" My first impression, or what I could see of it as my eyes adjusted to the dim light, was that it was a complete dump. The second was that we were sorely out of place; every pair of eyes landed on us, and they weren't friendly either.

"It's where the Fae and the wolves hang out when they are on our side and don't want to be near humans. I'm sure you'll recognize a lot of them."

As I scanned the room, I realized I did. "Should we be here, after what Vitor said?"

"This is my town. Nobody tells me where I can go." His hand on my back pushed me forward.

I nearly gagged on my first breath of heavy smoke filled the air. It didn't smell like pot, but it wasn't cigarettes either. Men and women lounged about as a weird song I'd never heard played loudly, thumping bass vibrating the floor. The men outnumbered the women by about two to one, and the females that were present all seemed to be coupled up. No little pockets of two or three girls grouped, like you'd expect to see in normal club.

"Why are there no single women?" I asked. I'd

always gotten a chauvinist vibe from the wolves and I was feeling vindicated and annoyed all at once.

"They only come here with men," he replied, having no idea how that would irritate me.

"Why? They can't be without a man?" My voice started to rise.

"Maybe at some point you can go over there and start a women's lib. Right now, I've got bigger concerns. That's my guy, in the corner."

I looked across the smoke filled room to the corner where a weird little man sat. "It figures you wouldn't care. You and your people, that's all you worry about."

His arm tightened around me as we changed direction suddenly. He yanked me into a dark nook and his body blocked out the room.

"This isn't the place." His words were serious but I refused to be put off.

"Easy for you to…"

"Stop and listen to me; half of the men in here would like to tear you from limb to limb for what you did to Tracker. They'd like to kill me for allowing it."

I knew he was right. I had also started to feel a sense of security when I was with him. No one ever messed with him, so if he was really concerned about that, he wouldn't have brought me here. "Why did you even bring me here?" I asked, as I realized there had to be another intent.

"Because I needed them to see you are off limits." He angled closer and I didn't know myself what he was about to do. His hand cupped the side of my head. The light bulb went off then. He was making it look like I wasn't just with him, I was *with* him. I just wish it felt as fake as it was supposed to be, instead of the close contact sending my hormones all into a tizzy.

I wanted him to lean closer at the same time I was afraid he'd do just that. In my nervousness, I started to blather, "Don't you guys have a news letter or some other means of getting the word out?"

"No, and even if we did," he leaned in close enough that I could feel the stubble on his face graze my neck, "it wouldn't be nearly as much fun as this."

Did he just nibble on my ear lobe?

He leaned his head back but his body still hovered close to mine. His eyes spoke volumes. This was quickly turning from a sham display into the real thing.

"So what else are we doing here?" I said, as I tried to steer this back into a safer zone. I was a touch disappointed when it worked and I saw his face grow serious again.

"The guy in the corner runs this place. He might have some answers."

He looked concerned. He had the same hunch I did: whoever this senator was, he was bad news. He finally stepped back and we headed over to the owner.

He was an odd little man with almost black hair, but not quite. Even in the dim light, a strange greenish highlight shimmered.

"Burrom," Cormac greeted the stumpy little man. Burrom simply nodded in the direction of a hallway off the back of the main room. He stood up from his stool, proving just how short he was. He was smoking a pipe with whatever strange tobacco was filling this place with a weird odor. It trailed behind as we followed him into a room that was surprisingly clean, compared to the club. Inside was a monitor, displaying a picture of the hallway and also several different vantage points of the club . A rustic looking table that appeared to serve as a desk sat in the corner with a single chair. It appeared he didn't do much entertaining in here.

"You know you're going to get me in hot water," Burrom finally spoke. His voice sounded surprisingly deep and mismatched for his size. "I don't get involved and I don't take sides."

"And you know you don't want to piss me off. Now, what do you know? And don't pretend you don't know what I'm talking about," Cormac said in his scary voice. At least I'd think it was his scary voice if I were Burrom.

"I don't know much. Just that he's not right. He only came in here once, with Tracker." He did a little hop to get himself seated upon the table.

"You know more than that." Cormac declared.

"It's only a hunch."

"Tell me." He took a step closer to Burrom. Cormac might have been trying to bully information out of him but I had the strange feeling he liked this small Fae.

"He's not one of us. And by that, I mean neither Fae or Werewolf."

"Why do you say that?" I asked.

Burrom hesitated for only a couple of seconds before he tried to explain. "When I met him,

Tracker said he was one of them, which I knew for a lie. I knew he wasn't pure Wolf but I figured he was some sort of relation and it was simply a stretch on the truth. We don't normally shake hands, that's a human thing, but he extended his hand to me. I thought he'd assimilated, but something niggled at me, so I threw up a blocker when I grasped his hand." He paused and looked directly to me, "It stops an inflow of energy," he explained and then continued, "I felt something odd. It wasn't a spell, but it sure as hell wasn't human or Wolf either. He was trying to do something to me."

"What?" I asked.

"I've got no idea." He shook his head and looked as frustrated by the lack of information as we were. You could tell he wasn't used to being in the dark on anything.

"Any guess what he might be?" I asked.

"No."

"You see him again or hear anything, you call me immediately," Cormac said.

Burrom nodded. We left his office and we headed out through the club. When the fresh night air hit my lungs, I couldn't take a breath deep enough to cleanse myself of the smog we'd just left. I watched Cormac's Ferrari pull up; the kid threw him his keys and disappeared as quickly as he had come.

I was just about to walk around to my side of the car when Cormac bum rushed me and tackled me to the ground. My body hit the pavement as I felt the burn of flesh as it was shaved off my body as I slid along the rough surface with two hundred plus pounds sliding on top of me. My first thought was to start yelling that just because I could take a beating didn't mean they should think it was okay to rough me up all the time. Before I could say anything, bullets whizzed past my head and ricocheted through the alley answering the question. His entire weight crushed down upon me.

"Cormac?" I asked, hoping the dead weight didn't mean what I thought.

Nothing.

"Cormac!" My voice sounded slightly hysterical to even me.

I didn't hear anymore bullets and I needed to get him out of there. From what I did know, Alchemists could take a beating, I knew that from personal experience. What I didn't know was how much of one. There were limits. Cormac had reminded me on several occasions that we could be killed.

As I felt the sticky warmth between our bodies, I knew that even with our capabilities, you still needed blood. If he bled out, it would be game over. I pushed at him with a strength I didn't know I had and rolled out from underneath him. I didn't wait even a second before I grabbed his arms and started to drag all six feet plus of him toward the passenger side of the car. If I hadn't had so much adrenaline pumping, I'm not sure I would have made it, but I had to get him out of the open. The car was the nearest cover in an alley where we were caught like fish in a barrel. When nothing shot at us again, I assumed the shooter had taken off.

I should've looked around, but I didn't, so intent

on dragging his lifeless body to the car. I was in pure reaction mode. Until a bullet whizzed so close to me I felt it move a lock of hair away from my face.

Then I saw him. The senator stood in the alley, about ten feet from me. Silver temples, accented dark hair. He was impeccably dressed in an expensive suit with cuff links that peaked out of the sleeves and shoes that gleamed. But no gun.

"That would be my sniper," he waved toward the rooftop of the building we had just come out of. I saw a man dressed in all black, complete with a ski mask, who stood there with a gun pointed on me. I looked down, a little red dot danced against the white of my shirt.

I let Cormac's arms fall to the ground and stepped in front of him to shield him from any more bullets, knowing he was hanging on by a thread.

"What do you want?" I had no other plan than to buy Cormac's body time to repair some of the damage.

"I want this world and I want you dead. All of you."

He was bluffing. If he wanted me dead, he'd have me shot right now. "Than do it."

"Not yet." He was gloating.

"What are you waiting for?" I goaded in anger. Have I mentioned I have more balls than brains?

"The right time. Payback." He smiled a sadistic smile.

"For what?" I couldn't understand the hatred I felt pouring out of him.

"Because you and your people made me and

47

then turned on me because you couldn't stand that I was superior," he sneered, as he lost some of his superior appearance and control.

"I didn't turn on anyone."

Another shot fired and I crouched over Cormac, thinking they were going to try and finish him off. I looked to the building top, and tried to locate the sniper and saw a man I thought was Burrom by his small stature. The small shape did a leaping arch that struck the sniper in the throat with an agility that surprised me. I'd be surprised if he hadn't crushed the sniper's windpipe. So much for questioning him afterward.

I made a move toward the senator and he jumped back away from me. He was afraid of me. Why? But before I could take another step, bullets rained at our feet.

I looked up to see Burrom with the gun.

"I don't know who you are," he called down from the rooftop, "but take your fight elsewhere."

The senator and I stared at each other as we both debated our options. My gut said Burrom wouldn't shoot me, but I felt torn in two. I wanted to pursue the senator but I didn't know how badly Cormac was injured. I stared at him for another second that Cormac didn't have and I saw him gloat.

I envisioned ripping him from limb to limb when in actuality I was running back to the car. I found the keys lying close to where we had gone down.

I looked up to the rooftop where Burrom still stood guard with the gun in his hand. He gave me a nod and indicated he had my back as I quickly - or as quickly as I could - dragged Cormac into the passenger side.

I jumped into the driver's seat, planning on running the bastard over if he was still standing there, but he was gone. I tried every button on the dash and steering wheel until I figured out how to get the Bluetooth working. "Call Dodd," I said, and hoped Cormac didn't have him stored under some weird pseudonym.

"Hey Boss. How'd it go?" I heard his deep voice answer.

"Not good." It took supreme concentration for me to keep the panic from my voice.

"Jo? Where's Cormac?"

The panic in Dodd's voice didn't help matters. "He's here with me...but barely."

"What do you mean? Why isn't he speaking?"

"He took some bullets and I think he might be bleeding out." I looked at Cormac's lifeless form.

"Does he have a pulse?"

I reached over with my right hand and tried to get a read, as I flew through the streets.

"Does he have a pulse?!" Dodd's voice filled the car as he screamed.

"I'm trying! Hold on!" My hands shook so badly it was hard to feel the faint pulse, but it was there. "Yes."

"Is he still bleeding?"

"I think so." I looked over at the pool of blood on the seat under his crumpled form and thought it looked larger than it had been.

"How far away are you?"

I knew this area like the back of my hand but I

still had to look at the street sign as my brain froze. "Only a couple of blocks away." I ground the car's gears as I tried to shift into fourth.

"Pull directly into his private garage. I'll make sure all the gates are open and I'll meet you there."

And then I was alone, or at least it felt like it. Cormac hadn't moved once. My brain replayed the scene and I couldn't remember how many bullets had been fired, maybe too many to count. I glanced over to where he was slumped against the seat and hoped he would start speaking. I'm not the squeamish type but I'd never seen so much blood come from anyone. Stop. Looking. Just drive…you're almost there. I gripped the steering wheel harder and pretended my hands weren't shaking.

I flew up the ramp into the private garage, everything was open, just as promised. Standing in front of the door, only about ten feet from my trailer, stood Dodd, Dr. Sabrina, who I remembered from the night I'd gotten radiation overdose, Buzz and Ben. I drove the last couple of feet before I hit the brakes.

Dodd had Cormac out of the car before I'd even screeched to a complete stop.

"Lay him down and sit right here, Dodd," the doctor instructed as she kneeled next to him without a thought to the pretty white sun dress she wore.

A tube was already hanging from Dodd's vein and the doctor inserted it into Cormac's arm a second later.

"Well?" Dodd asked, the first of us to utter the question.

She felt his pulse, opened his lids and gazed into his eyes with a light. "We're good."

"Should we move him?" Ben chimed in, as we all looked at Cormac, lifeless on the ground.

"I wouldn't bother. He'll be up soon enough. With the new injection of blood, he'll be standing on his own in another ten minutes."

I felt the tension slip away like a storm wind blowing in after a boiling summer day, bringing a new set of issues with it.

"What happened?" It was clear Dodd instinctively took charge when Cormac couldn't, and his ease in the position made me wonder how often that was.

I gave them all a quick recap as Dodd grilled me for details I couldn't answer.

"This doesn't make sense. How could a sniper have snuck up on Cormac? He smells a sniper from ten miles away. There has to be more. What were you doing?" They all stared at me.

"I don't know how. He just did. That's all I remember," I said defensively. Why was everyone looking at me as if it was my fault?

"And when you pulled away, the senator was just gone?" Dodd continued to interrogate me.

"Yes. Can you grill me later after we know he's okay?" I asked, I was still uneasy at the sight of him lying there. I had an irrational urge to kick him and scream at him to sit up.

"Relax. Doc gave us the thumbs up." I saw him look over at my trailer. "Hey, do you have any beer in there?"

I threw my hands up, aghast at the question.

"No, I don't."

"That sucks. Okay, so you thought he was scared of you?" The last question had a tone I found hard not to be insulted by.

"Yes. I think he was scared of me." I spoke a bit slower to get my point across.

"If that was the case, why didn't you take a shot at him?" He shifted in his spot still seated next to Cormac.

Sabrina knelt down next to the two of them and started to withdraw the transfusion of Dodd's blood.

"I didn't try to take a shot because of your almost dead friend? Burrom, on the roof, with a gun aimed at us?"

Sabrina looked at me as I talked with my hands as I became more and more agitated.

"Do you want me to take a look at those?" she asked, looking directly at where my sleeve hung, shredded.

I held up my arm and got a good look at the road burn already scabbed and healing. "No, I'm fine."

"I think you could've gotten *one* good blow in," Dodd said, having trouble letting the subject drop.

"He was bleeding out on the pavement."

"Look, no judgment here, I just think I could've pulled off at least one shot is all," he replied, clearly passing judgment.

"Leave her alone," Cormac said and startled me from my annoyance at Dodd. All eyes fell to him as he started to sit up, not even eight minutes after I'd pulled in. Were the doctor's calculations wrong or was he just one tough S.O.B.? I'd guessed the latter.

He was on his feet a minute later, looking l a hundred percent, other than the fact he was wearing clothes soaked in blood, riddled with bullet holes, that is.

"He disappeared completely?" Cormac asked as he took off his bloodied shirt.

"Yes. You heard all of that?" I asked, a bit startled. Did his brain work better than mine? He'd just almost died blocking bullets meant for me; was it wrong to feel jealous?

"Nothing? Not a trace?"

"Yes. That's what I said." I looked at him, so sure on his feet. He was the picture of health again.

"Dodd, call Burrom and find out what he saw." Then he turned toward me. "You. Don't leave this casino." I watched him walk from the garage.

I've never been good at following directions. All you have to do is look at my Ikea bureau with the crooked drawers to figure that one out.

CHAPTER FIVE

"So what do you think?" Lacey asked.

"Huh?"

"Jo! You need to pay attention! I just can't figure him out," Lacey complained as she lounged on my couch, feet on the armrest, while she waited for her toenails to dry.

I looked down at my phone again. I called Rick the moment Cormac left yesterday, in hopes of setting up a meeting. It was two in the afternoon the next day and still no call back? I was starting to think he wasn't that anxious to see me.

"Jo! Stop staring at your phone and help me!"

"I'm sorry. What's the problem with Cormac?" I left my phone on the counter and plopped down on my couch with her. I'd hear it ring, staring at it wouldn't do anything for me.

"I swear you don't listen to me. He's acting all buddy buddy with me."

"And?" I asked trying to figure out the

problem.

"I don't want to be his buddy." A pout appeared on her face.

"I thought you said you were okay with just being friends? You didn't even used to want to be in the same room with him." I knew she'd been either lying to me or herself, but I couldn't help point it out.

"That was when I thought he was scary. But then he seemed...I don't know, not as scary? Plus, you've seen him."

Yes, a bit too much, but it was a little late to come clean on that. I'd always been so good at secrets but all I wanted to do now was spill the entire story to Lacey. I wouldn't. I was too afraid. The way things were getting so weird around here, what if that contract actually had some juice? And if I didn't tell her any of the weird stuff, it was going to be hard to explain the kiss. How do I tell her that I couldn't date the hot rich guy because he shot me in the head? She'd think I was a nut, because if I got shot, how am I still alive? And if I did blow my promise all to pieces then I'd have to hear it for even kissing the guy that had me shot. Nah, some things were better off as secrets.

"Yeah, he's cute," I said trying to act disinterested.

"You need glasses if you think he's just cute. There is something about him that makes me just want to jump him. I swear, we were that close a couple of wccks ago." She held up her fingers demonstrating for me. "Arnold asked me to run something up into his place. I got there and I was trying to chat him up and use my wiles on him. At first, I didn't think it was going to work, but then all of a sudden he's all 'come sit next to me' and stuff. Even put his hand on my leg. A minute later, he said he had to go and was giving me the bum's rush out. That was it. Nothing. Not even a hot kiss to show for it. Now we're in some weird yucky friend zone and I don't like it."

"Did he say anything about it? The night you thought he was interested?" I looked at my nails, feigning interest.

"Nothing, like it never happened. He's not always even that nice to me. Never mean, just disinterested."

She lay there for a second, and I could tell she wanted to say something that she felt uncomfortable with. I just waited.

Finally, it came out. "This is going to sound stupid, but I think he's nicer to me when you're there," she shot out quickly. "What do you make of that?"

I wanted to talk but I couldn't. Her big brown eyes stared at me, and I could see all she wanted was for me to tell her she was be mistaken. Because, if he was doing that, it meant he was just be using Lacey to get to me and we both knew it.

My phone started to buzz on the counter and I jumped for it and not just because I wanted to speak to Rick anymore.

"Desperate much?" Lacey said as I grabbed it and hit the answer button and held it to my ear.

"Caitlin?" the voice on the other side said.

"Hi, yes!"

"I'm so happy you called! I just got my phone back on. I dropped it in a puddle and I've been running from event to event. I just got it replaced and heard your message."

"I was wondering if you wanted to grab a bite to eat? Catch up a little? I've got a break in about an hour."

I saw Lacey's intent face and she mouthed *'who is that'?*

'Old friend,' I mouthed back.

'Cute?'

I nodded. He was cute, I wasn't lying.

"Perfect. Just tell me where," Rick said with enthusiasm.

He named a café on the strip that had outdoor seating. I agreed and hung up, already feeling guilty. I wasn't using him. I would want to see him even if he didn't have a connection to the senator, but I couldn't let an opportunity like this pass, either. We didn't know what he was and Rick was someone that had close contact.

My mind drifted back to the day Rick had given me the book of Monet prints I still had. It was the first gift I'd ever received that hadn't been an obligatory doll. It was as priceless to me as the real Monet Cormac had given me, after I'd gotten sick, that hung above my bed .

It took me ten minutes to appease Lacey's curiosity and get her out the door and another ten to pull myself together. It wasn't a date, and I felt a little bad letting Laccy think it might be. I felt worse about meeting him for his connection to the senator. He was one of the few people I held fond memories of and the idea of using him, in any sense, bothered me.

The place I was meeting him was only a couple of blocks away but I had to get out of the casino unseen first. No one ever said I was being watched, but I didn't seem to be able to leave the casino without a tail showing up.

The ramp. My guess is Cormac had people posted near the doors that kept tabs on me, but I doubted they were watching the ramp out.

The last thing I wanted was for Cormac to come to this get together. As much as we were supposed to be working together, my past wasn't an area I was ready to lay open for anyone. I didn't know what tidbits might slip out if he were there with me. Who would I even tell Rick he was? There were things about my past I wasn't ready to open up about, things that Rick had knowledge of.

It was a bit odd, making my way down the four story ramp designed for cars, but it was the best way out. I tried to duck near the sides every time I noticed a camera. Most of them appeared to be pointed toward the dead center of the ramp but I didn't know how wide a shot the lens might have.

Fifteen minutes later, I was searching the café for Rick. As I scanned the crowd, he stood up and waved me over to the table he had claimed in the bustling restaurant. A large, striped canopy shielded most of the patrons sitting at the tables. I walked over and before I knew what he was going to do, I was enveloped in the warmest hug I'd ever received.

"It's so great to see you," he said, still hugging me.

"You too," I said and meant it, hugging him back. We let go and I settled into the wrought iron seat across from him.

"I ordered some food. I hope your tastes are still the same," he said, motioning toward the food in front of me. That was Rick. He hadn't ordered it to rush the lunch, he had ordered it to show he still remembered, and prove what I had meant to him. I looked down to see a turkey club on the table. It had been eight years and he never forgot.

"So, tell me what you've been up to? You look fantastic."

"Just finished up my four year degree at UNLV. I'm thinking about Med school but decided to take a year off in between." I sipped my ice tea.

"That's really wonderful, Caitlin."

It was so strange to hear that name, from what felt like a lifetime ago. "So how are things going with you?"

"I've been with the senator for about a year now."

"Political life?" Sitting across café table from me in his navy blue suit with lapel pin, he looked the part.

"Yes, but with the best of intentions."

"I'd never think anything else." I wasn't lying. He'd always helped anyone he could. As refined as he seemed now, he'd been a tough kid but never a bully. When we had lived with the same family for four months it had been the only time I'd ever felt safe.

I felt slightly skittish even bringing up the senator, but this was my opening. "Do you like working for the senator?"

"Oh yeah! He's great! And honest. I truly believe in him." He took a bite of his burger, not rattled in the least by my interest.

"I read in the paper he's a local, from right here in Vegas?" Which I knew had to be total crap. Humans didn't traverse wormholes like it was a stroll in the park.

"Oh yeah," he nodded. "He still lives here with his wife and three kids." He waved his hand northward. "I can't remember the name of the development but it's about three miles north of here.

I knew the house he was talking about, or Cormac did. The senator hadn't been there in weeks. This was a waste of time. Why did I even come? He was buying into the senator's show - hook, line and sinker. What had happened to the kid I had known, that could see through any con you threw at him? And I'd know. I'd tried a couple out on him when we first met. Was he working with him? Could he have changed that much? I finished my meal, listening to the mundane minutia of his daily routine with the senator, attempting to appear like I wasn't disappointed. As he continued, I tried to get even a small hint of the truth behind the façade, but nothing was forthcoming. He believed everything he was saying. Worse, I think he believed everything the senator said.

I'd loved seeing Rick, even though I knew I couldn't see him again. My life was too crazy now and his proximity to the senator was too close to risk, but I lied and told him we'd do it again. We hugged each other goodbye, and I held on a little too tightly and for too long, knowing that this might be the last time I saw him. Knowing exactly who he'd be in close quarters with.

I was walking out of the gated eating area when he called my name. I turned, expecting him to tell me I had left something behind and was already feeling in my purse for my phone.

There Rick stood, about ten feet away from me. "Did I forget something?"

He stood smiling at me and when I took a step toward him he finally spoke.

"The senator says hello."

I stared at him and froze. He smiled like nothing was amiss. I was so shocked, I didn't see the gun until it was against his head, blowing his brains all over the café.

People stood screaming and crying as he lay in a pool of his own blood. I didn't rush over to him, I just stood there. I could see the gaping hole in his skull, even from where I was. And that was all I did as the chaos went on around me. Stood there for what felt like forever, the senator's words in the alley echoing in my brain.

An arm wrapped around my waist, half dragging, half carrying me out of there. "Come on, snap out of it," I heard Cormac say.

My legs moved but I was in a trance. One of the few people that I'd ever trusted had just blown a hole in his own head. And it was because of me. The senator was trying to get at me, at us.

A new black Ferrari was waiting not even a block away and he opened the door and pushed me into the passenger side. The force of the car taking off, seconds later, pressed me further into the seat.

"When was the last time you saw him?"

"Huh?" I knew Cormac had just spoken to me but I couldn't process anything. I felt mentally frozen on the image of Rick, while my body felt sapped of all strength as I sat there limp. "I've got to go back there."

"Not a good idea."

"I've got to go back. They'll need someone to identify him. I can't just leave him there, a nameless body." I reached for the car door, even though we were moving; I was intent on getting back to do something for Rick, even if it was just the last simple deed of naming the dead.

Cormac's arm pulled me back against the seat, his arm barring me from leaving the car.

"Jo, don't lose it on me here. I'm sure he had ID on him. Going back there will just link you to this. I can't have your face on the news."

His logic penetrated the haze and I nodded.

"You need to tell me everything you can about what just happened." I felt the car turning this way and that, but didn't care where he was driving.

"Oh god, Cormac, I don't know. It was so normal and I was so happy to see him doing well for himself. I know it was working for the senator …but it just didn't matter. People that come out of the life we had don't normally do well. He had pulled himself up and was working toward a career in politics." I shook off an image of his lapel pin, covered in blood.

"What happened? I saw you walk away and then turn back. You need to tell me what happened." He voice was very monotone compared to how it usually sounded.

"He called my name, I turned and he said 'the senator says hello' and then…he was smiling when he did it." I rolled down the window, looking for air. "I've got to get out of this car. Pull over." I leaned my face into the wind.

"I can't."

"I need to get out this car and …I don't know, I need to… Just pull over." Logic had returned enough for me to know it wouldn't look good if I jumped out of the moving car, even if I would be fine.

"I can't. That's the senator, in the silver Mercedes, about half a block up. He was watching the entire thing." My eye flew over the cars in front of us until I found the one he meant. I saw the back of his head. He was alone.

"Stop! Why are we following him? We don't even know what he's capable of."

"Because we need to know where he's going. We have to follow him."

"Why? Why us?" I already knew what he was going to say. I knew all the reasons, I just didn't want to.

He turned toward me as we waited at a light, still in the heart of the Strip.

"Forget the fact that I think this is somehow intrinsically attached to you, in a way neither of us can fathom, we are the only ones that can."

"No, I don't want this life."

He grabbed my chin and pulled my face in his direction when I refused to look at him. "Then why did you blow up that wormhole in the mountain?"

"I didn't have a choice." How could he not understand the difference? "I don't want to chase bad guys. I want out of this. I never asked to be a hero."

"The best ones never do," he replied in a soft voice and brushed his fingers across my cheek before he dropped his hand from my face. "Listen to me, a normal human won't even comprehend what's happening, let alone try to stop it. The wolves were involved with him, and might still be. The Fae? They care only about the Fae. If it doesn't touch them, they won't do a thing. Not until it threatens their life in some way. And even then, it's debatable. Vitor knew what was going down on the mountain that day. What did he do? Nothing."

"How did you know I was at the café with Rick?" I rubbed my hands on the skirt I was wearing, annoyed with their moistness and what it represented.

"You mean other than watching you walk down the car ramp for about ten minutes? Lacey told me."

I just shook my head and sighed.

"Don't be annoyed. She was excited for you. Said you hadn't had a date the entire time she's known you."

He sounded just a touch too happy about that and it annoyed me, especially right now after what had just happened. No one was allowed to be happy as waves of anger at what had just happened to Rick churned and built inside me. "Remember, I don't tell Lacey everything. You, of all people, should know that." I watched the Mercedes up ahead. "You don't think that was because of me, do you?" As the shock ebbed away, the reality of his death crept in close on its heels.

"Do you want the ugly truth?"

"Warts and all." I wasn't even sure why I asked. I already knew the answer.

"Then yes, I think it was to get at you."

I had expected the truth from him. He wasn't a sugar coater.

"But why? Because I kicked him into a wormhole? He made it out fine. He said I, we, turned on him, but I never even knew him." Him was still several cars in front of us.

"I don't know. If I've learned one thing in this world, I don't ignore my gut feelings. And my gut is screaming that this - whatever he is - we haven't even seen the beginning of what he's capable of."

I watched him open the Ferrari up as we headed off the main part of the strip. I knew he was trying to release some of the energy he had pent up inside. I knew he was as angry as I was, but I wasn't sure if it was for the same reasons. After he'd been shot by the sniper, he'd seemed concentrated but not this angry.

As far as Rick went, I suspected Cormac had killed his fair share of people. Hell, he'd tried to kill me. This anger wasn't just about Rick either.

"Don't get too close to him! He'll spot us."

"I know a little bit about this."

I leaned back in my seat as we hit the desert and tried to clear my mind. "Rick never would have shot himself, ever. He was tough. But what kind of thing could make him do that?"

"I believe you. I've seen people lose it. He wasn't on the edge. His movements, even right up to the end, didn't show any strain."

My head snapped in his direction. "How long were you there?"

"Does it matter?" He didn't bother looking at me.

"Yes. It's creepy." How could he not know that?

"I wasn't just watching you two, I was watching the senator watch you."

My skin crawled at the thought of the senator watching us as well. "Thanks. That just upped the creepy factor another notch."

"And I thought we agreed we were working as a team on this?"

Now he looked at me. I guess this he deemed important. I wondered when he'd get to that.

"I needed to do this solo."

"Why?"

"Because I did. Look, I've never done a team effort before, on anything, so you are going to have to cut me some slack here and there." I hoped that was going to be good enough because I wasn't going to elaborate any further.

He turned his full attention back to the road and didn't say anything else.

"Why would he be heading to California?" I asked as I saw the sign quickly approaching.

The tires screeched and I banged into the side of the door as Cormac jerked the wheel and we skidded and swung around.

"What's wrong?" The car finally came to a stop

on the opposite shoulder, facing the other direction.
I thanked god there hadn't been any other cars.

"What the hell is wrong with you? You say we
have to follow him, and sell me on all this hero shit,
and now we're losing him?" I watched the senator's
car shrink from a dot on the horizon to nothing. I
knew he was right. We had to get the bastard or
who knew what would come next. Even if I wasn't
ready for a full blown confrontation, I still wanted
to know where he was going. We needed
information and Cormac had stopped in the middle
of the best tail we'd had?

He grabbed the key from the ignition and
stepped out of the car, holding his phone.

"Cormac! What the hell are you doing! We
don't have time for a phone call," I screamed, as I
followed him out.

He held up a finger in a motion for me to give
him a minute. I eyed the keys in his hand but I knew
I didn't have a shot at getting them from him. Then I
eyed the car. In my teens, I'd hotwired a car or two.
Okay, maybe more like a couple of hundred, and I
wondered if I still had the skills, if cars were still
wired the same.

I walked back to the car as casually as I could,
while he talked to whoever was so goddamn
important that we were losing the senator. I was a
foot away when he swooped in quicker than I'd ever
seen him move and shut the doors, the lock
sounding as I looked on. I would've taken a swing at
him, I was so pissed, but he was already ten feet
away, still on the phone.

"I don't want to be partnered with you

anymore!" I yelled in his direction. "You suck at this!"

Aggravated beyond words, I started walking in the direction of California. I knew it was stupid. I knew I wasn't going to be able to catch the senator on foot but with having no other option, I couldn't stop the compulsion of at least moving in the right direction.

I'd taken only three steps before I found myself dangling over Cormac's shoulder as we both retreated from the border.

I tried to punch him in the kidneys but it didn't even slow him as the jerk still talked on the phone. "No, keep looking. It's in there. Ow! That hurt," he said, as I grabbed a fistful of his hair. "No, I'm not talking to you. Just keep looking."

"What are you doing?" I demanded. I took another shot at his back.

"Okay, now look at line six. You've got to undo that," he said, ignoring the blows I rained upon him.

He dropped me onto the ground about twenty feet away, just as I got a good bite at his left tricep.

"Don't move," he said.

Ignoring him, I both stood and moved. When I moved right, so did he. Same thing when I went left.

"It's done? Good." He shoved his phone back in his pocket and then stepped out of my way.

"You better tell me what is going on right now, *partner*." I squinted my eyes and took the most threatening pose I could.

"I'd prefer not to," he responded, unfazed by my scary posture. He strolled back to the car and leaned against it.

"Tell me anyway," I said as I followed him.

"We should talk about this on the way back."

I crossed my arms and shook my head. "Tell me now."

"You're not going to like it." He grimaced a little. "Remember the first contract you signed?"

"Yes," I said as I thought back to it. "It only stated that I couldn't repeat anything."

"But I told you that you couldn't leave the area."

I shook my head. "That wasn't on the contract. I remember every line. It was only about repeating things."

"Just because you didn't see it, doesn't mean it wasn't on there. I told you specifically that you couldn't leave the area." He said it in a manner that laid the blame for this mishap on me. "The state line served as the boundary."

"What would have happened if I'd have crossed the border into California?" I took a couple steps in that direction to accent my point and because I was getting so angry it was hard to stand still.

He rubbed he shadow on his jaw. "It would've been pretty painful."

"Would it have killed me?"

"No, it just would've hurt like hell."

I marched up to him, mad as hell and letting it show in every step I took. "I want those papers destroyed when we get back." I shoved his shoulder. Or tried, it didn't actually budge him.

"Not all things are reversible."

"What's that mean?"

"It means that some of the things can't be taken back."

"Just how screwed am I?"

"Don't talk to humans and alls good. For the most part."

"I want everything that can be undone destroyed by today."

He nodded. "Done. I will undo everything I can."

He turned and opened the car door for me and waited for me to get in. I paused by the door, and thought that he'd relented to easily.

"I'll do it," he said again.

I nodded and got in the car. We started to drive back, the senator long gone.

Now that the chase was over, Rick's image floated into my head again. When someone says that something is burned into their brain, it's not far from the truth. The mind isn't like a computer, with a fixed anatomy, but changes throughout our life. Seeing Rick die today had changed a part of my brain. That image would be with me forever.

"If we are going to take this thing down, we need to know what it is," I said with a new conviction.

"Agreed."

"We need information, and the only place I've heard of there being records is with the wolves. We need it."

"They aren't going to just hand it over."

"Then we take it."

CHAPTER SIX

"Sure you're ready?" Cormac asked as he eyed my sneakers. He had told me to wear hiking boots but I drew the line at tennis shoes.

"Cormac, how many times are you going to ask me that?" I went on the offensive before he commented on my jeans.

"The air is going to be thinner."

"You told me."

"And it's darker."

"Whatever, it is doesn't matter because we aren't going to be there long." I hoped.

"Dodd, Buzz...give us a minute." They'd been lingering in the back of the room, waiting to see us off.

I watched as they both left the portal room.

Cormac stood, hovering slightly, dressed all in black. "You aren't taking this seriously. It can get rough over there very quickly. On this side, there is at least the pretention of civility. Over there, in the wolves' territory at least," he pointed to where the wormhole would open, "you piss them off and they just kill you."

I laughed a little. "Yes, that's so much different to what I've experienced here," I said making an obvious reference to them trying to kill me.

Cormac didn't laugh. "Take this seriously or I'll take Dodd instead."

"Relax, I get it. Let's just get on with it already." I knew he wouldn't go without me but I didn't feel like spending the next twenty minutes arguing about it.

"You think you're tough, but you don't know what's out there."

"I think I've got an idea."

He shook his head. "You stay by me the whole time. You don't leave unless I say so. And if I do tell you to leave, you do exactly as I say."

"Who made you boss? I thought we were partners?"

"That's the only reason I'm even letting you come." He took a couple of steps toward the door to call back Buzz and Dodd.

"That and I'm probably the only one that can open a wormhole up from the other side in a hurry," I said.

That stopped him in his tracks as he looked back to me. "Goddamn it, Buzz can't keep his mouth shut." He sighed audibly and opened the door as the guys walked back in.

"What?" Buzz asked as Cormac shot him a look.

"Must you repeat everything to her?" he asked, still scowling.

"It's not my fault. She said I owed her. It was either tell her or she was going to hit me over the head when I least expected it."

I covered my mouth with my hand to hide my smile, not wanting to gloat.

"Forget it. We're going in. I'll open, then you guys shut it behind us," Cormac said as he walked away from Dodd.

I stood back and watched as Cormac opened up a portal. I wasn't sure if it was because he was older and more experienced or because he was strong, but it was flawless. He opened it just large enough for two people to walk through and the edges didn't fluctuate even a smidge. That might sound like nothing, but we were talking about warping the space time fabric of our very existence. That's some heavy shit to be able to pull off seamlessly.

He looked toward me and held out his hand. "You ready?"

"Yes." The adrenaline pumped through my veins as I moved toward him. In less than a minute, I'd be on a different planet. How many people could say that? Actually, I wasn't even going to be able to say that. Damn contract took all the fun out of things. Half the joy of doing some stuff is being able to talk about it after.

Oh well, this was still the coolest thing I'd ever done in my life. It was scary as hell, but cool. I was going to travel through a wormhole to steal documents from a group of werewolf aliens. I felt like a live wire as energy pumped through me.

Maybe I was made for this hero stuff. Maybe this was what I was meant to do. Maybe I should keep the hero thoughts to myself until I made it back in one piece.

I'd stepped into this wormhole countless times, but I'd never gone further than a few steps beyond the entrance. The lavender sky became more brilliant the closer I got.

"They won't see us stepping out?" I asked as we neared the other side.

"No, this opens to an empty area. They are a superstitious lot. They think that living too close to this energy could affect them negatively," he replied from slightly in front of me.

Cormac stepped out first and I watched, a small part of me afraid he'd fry on the spot, but he didn't. I took a deep breath and my first step into a different universe. The ground was slightly springy, covered with a moss-like surface that was a turquoise color. Trees, or what would've been trees on Earth, hovered higher than I'd ever seen, bigger than even redwoods, like sky scrapers. But the thing I noticed the most was the sweet, cloying scent on the air as I breathed deeply.

Cormac stood close by and watched my slow adjustment. "You'll get used to it. The oxygen level is lower, but it's not dangerous."

I nodded, not willing to waste my air on speaking yet as the feeling of not being able to get enough was threatening a bit of a panic. He grabbed the backpack off my shoulders and threw it over his, now carrying two. I would've argued but I was too grateful to pick a fight about my independence.

"Come on, I want to get deeper under cover. The area isn't occupied but that doesn't mean we can't be spotted."

I followed him sluggishly as he moved around the larger trees.

"Do you know where we're going?" I asked as I realized I had no idea.

"You just thought of that now?"

He annoyed me just enough to waste my oxygen. "I wouldn't talk. If your people hadn't been paranoid freaks and destroyed every ounce of history, we wouldn't be here."

He stopped in his tracks. "How many times do I have to remind you that they're your paranoid freaks as well? And yes, I do know where we are going. I don't need a map. I've been there before."

"So where is it exactly?" I looked ahead, nothing but trees as far as I could see.

"We've got a two mile hike ahead of us." He started back in the same direction we'd been going.

"And you don't think the place is guarded?" I asked, staring at his back.

"This isn't one of the main settlements. They'll have people in the area, but I don't think too many. The Fae have no interest in their records and wouldn't bother. I don't think they'll have any idea that we would try to take them."

"Are you sure asking wouldn't have worked?" I asked. I tugged on the backpack he was carrying and we stopped. I dug through my pack and grabbed a water bottle, taking a swig.

"I know you haven't talked to too many of them, but what do you think?" He raised his eyebrows.

No answer was needed. I stopped talking, not wanting to waste anymore of my air on it and we started back through the trees. Suddenly, the area cleared. When he had said hike, he'd really meant it. The ridiculously wide trees had blocked the rocky hill that lay ahead of us.

As we started to climb a craggy surface, I bit back a small yelp which turned into a larger squeal as my foot slipped on some moss, interspersed here and there just to make traveling the rocks that much more unpleasant.

"You okay?" Cormac asked, as he doubled back a few feet to check out the nasty gash that bled down my leg. The sharp rocks had cut right through my jeans.

"Yeah, I'm fine." I looked up at the rest of the way ahead. "Can't we float or something?"

"Alchemists can float but it's an up down thing, we don't move forward."

"That just sucks."

"At least I *can* float." He seemed a bit insulted over my comment.

"What's that supposed to mean? I've floated. You've seen me."

He took a step back and stared at me. "Go ahead, float. I dare you."

I shrugged. "Maybe I don't feel like floating right now."

"Not to take anything from you, you are exceptional at opening wormholes, but you seem to have deficits in other areas." He kept moving forward as he talked and I had to scramble to keep

76

up.

"Are you calling me slow?"

"More like an idiot savant." I couldn't see his face but I could sense the smile on his face from the change in the tone of his words.

"Then what are you? You needed me here to be able to make sure you could even get back."

"I also didn't get stuck to a ceiling."

I opened my mouth but he beat me to the punch.

"I know why you carry that nickel around."

"That, sir, was a low blow." I raised my chin to the air and pushed past him up the slope without looking back.

I could feel him behind me. I always felt him when he was close by; it wasn't a comforting feeling, no, not comforting at all. It made me conscious of every move I made. If I didn't have a point to prove, I would've let him take the lead again. We'd see who was slow.

It took us about another twenty minutes to reach the top. Lying on our stomachs, we peered over the cliff at the valley below. I could tell it was a town, of sorts, but like nothing I'd ever seen. The same gigantic trees lined the perimeter of an area that looked to be several miles in diameter. What I thought were huge boulders turned out to be buildings as I watched people walk in and out of carved doorways.

"What we need is supposed to be in that one," he pointed toward the middle.

"The one in the dead center?" It was surrounded by at least fifty other stone-like structures in the heart of all the activity.

"Yes."

"The place is crawling with people." At least they were all in human form. I remembered what Tracker had looked like that night in the basement which seemed so long ago now. He hadn't looked like a wolf, but a monster. Seeing them walk around in human form was much more comforting. "Do they ever go to sleep?"

"In about eight hours they'll start. They don't sleep much, but they sleep like the dead when they do.

"We couldn't come any earlier. The light from the wormhole is too bright. Even several miles away, it can be seen at night. It wasn't safe." Cormac shimmied a few feet back from the edge and tugged on my ankle to get me to follow him as we settled in to wait it out.

When I awoke sometime later, I noticed the air had gotten chillier and that I was snug up against something very warm and hard. My arm was draped across his ridged stomach and my leg draped over his thighs. It was my traitorous subconscious who took over as I slept and clearly couldn't get enough physical contact with this man. I lay there for a moment while I tried to decide how to detach myself without waking him.

"How was your nap?"

Too late. His deep voice reverberated through me since I was lying pretty much on top of him.

"It's quite chilly now," I replied as I sat up, not having the nerve to look at him as I detached. I looked up and saw the massive moon hanging above us. I'd seen glimpses of it from the other end of the wormhole a few times, but didn't realize just how large it would be. In person, it was awe inspiring.

While I straightened myself and tugged my hair back into a ponytail, I watched Cormac walk over to the edge.

"Are you ready to do this?" he asked as he came back over.

"Yes. Let's do it. How do we get down there?" I started looking for a trail of some sort.

"We're going to float down."

"I can't float reliably, remember?"

"I'll float us both down."

I peeked back over the edge of what had to be a five hundred foot drop. "Are you sure you can float two people? That's a whole hell of a way down."

"You're going to have to trust me on this."

"You drop me and this partnership is through."

"I've never dropped a girl by accident, only on purpose," he said, and smirked as he dug out a bag he'd stashed in one of the backpacks.

"What's that for?"

"Supplies we might need to steal stuff." He took a step closer. "Put your arms around me."

"Is this the brightest way to go in?" I asked, having second thoughts. "Maybe we should take a less direct path in?"

"We could meander in slow and steady, but sometimes hard and fast is best."

I couldn't look down, and now I couldn't look at him either. He was probably talking about the matter at hand, but I wasn't really sure. I just wish it hadn't sounded so sexual while I was draped over him for the second time in less than an hour.

We stepped to the edge and took a final look down. Actually, I only looked for a second because my fear of heights was already starting to get the best of me, but from what I saw, nothing and no one stirred. He pushed off with his foot and we slowly started to float down. We both wore black but if anyone woke and looked, they'd be able to spot us in the light this giant moon reflected.

We hit the ground silently a few moments later and I followed him quickly to the side of one boulder. I could see door openings but none of them had windows. Cormac grabbed my hand as we moved, boulder by boulder, closer to the center of the area until we were at the one that supposedly housed information. It was the largest by far, with about a thirty foot radius.

We circled until we came to the door, or sort of door. It was simply a flap of leather that hung down over the opening, like the rest of the buildings. Cormac turned and held up a hand and mouthed for me to 'wait there.' I nodded in agreement and then followed immediately behind him anyway. Would he never learn? If I hadn't wanted to not get caught, I would've laughed.

When we entered, it was pitch black inside; I couldn't see a thing and walked straight into Cormac's back.

"I thought I told you to wait?" he whispered to

me.

"You did. How are we going to find anything?"

I heard him rustling in front of me as he pulled out a very dim flashlight and handed me another. I held it up, scanning the walls and my breath caught. It was lined, from floor to domed ceiling, all with books. Shit! Getting in had been the easy part. Finding the stuff we wanted was going to take forever.

I quickly scanned the spines of the closest books to me.

"Cormac, nothing is in English. How are we supposed to know which ones we need?"

"It'll say Keepers or Alchemists on it in English, at least that's what Vitor told me." He dug in his pocket and pulled out a slip of paper. "And this is how Book of Omens is written."

I took the slip from his hand and looked at the strangle symbols. "It's here?"

"It's rumored to have been taken by the wolves. It could be." We split up them as we both started at a different end of the room.

I'd always had a soft spot for Vitor but it was quickly hardening as we stood in the middle of an enemy camp on his planet while he frolicked, all safe and sound, on mine. I was going to have to remember this next time he whined about his people. Yeah, yeah, whatever. My people are blowing holes in their heads. Where the hell is he?

I scanned book after book, searching for some sign and was starting to completely doubt Vitor. Had he ever even seen these books? I looked at the top shelves I couldn't reach and that's when I noticed Cormac was floating along the top perimeter. I closed my eyes and tried to float but nothing. It sucked. If I had a mental block as a normal human, I could just go see a therapist but how the hell would I explain it to one? *Hi Doc. I'm frustrated about not floating.*

I wandered over to him, having perused the lower shelves to no use.

"Here," he said, pausing his light on one book. "I think this is something." He lifted his hand to pull the book out but I grabbed his ankle that was nearest my shoulder.

"What?" he asked looking down at me.

"Doesn't this seem a little too easy to you?"

He hung there for a moment, not moving. "Yes, but I'm not leaving empty handed."

"I'm just getting this weird foreboding feeling." I thought I was probably being paranoid. Things didn't have a tendency to work out smoothly in my experience. "Forget it. Let me see what you found."

He grabbed the book and no sooner did he pull it from the shelf did he jerk back his hand in pain. If it had only been that, we still might have been okay but the shelf he pulled it from let out a high pitched squealing noise, a type I'd never heard, high, loud and piercing. The gig was up. We had minutes, perhaps just seconds before the entire village came for us and we were stuck in a building with only one entrance.

Cormac dropped to the ground as I went to pick up the book. I wasn't prepared to leave empty handed either. The minute I touched it, a piercing pain shot through my hand and down my arm. It felt like someone was simultaneously breaking my bones while setting fire to me all at once.

Cormac grabbed it next, and I don't know how he managed, but he held onto it long enough to get it into the bag he carried. He held the bag outstretched in one hand while he grabbed mine in the other and we raced toward the door.

The second he pulled back the flap, I knew we were in trouble. Men and women in different phases of mutating were already outside and starting to run in our direction. I didn't stop to count as we took off back toward where we opened the wormhole before, but my guess was about twenty chased us and another ten were in front of us.

"What are we going to do?" I screamed as Cormac kept running toward the ten in front of us pulling me along with him.

"Just stay close to me and don't let go."

Having no other good idea or option myself, I ran beside him. He had a death grip on my hand that felt like it was a hair away from breaking my fingers, but I wasn't going to complain. I'd take a handful of broken fingers if he could get us the hell out of this mess. The men heading straight at us didn't look curious, they looked pissed. They also didn't look even an iota human anymore. Several feet taller, their elongated jaws held sharp teeth with lips curled up in growls. They knew where we had been and they wanted us dead. I didn't even want to look at the angry mob behind us. If those things got a hold of us, we'd be torn to pieces in minutes.

I felt a shimmer of energy pulse for less than a second before the group in front of us was upon us and as we plowed through them, I realized it for what it was: Cormac had put up some sort of shield. They tried to grab at him but they couldn't seem to. They were just shoved out of the way as if he were in some sort of invisible balloon suit.

I wasn't so lucky as I felt hands grab at me. The parts closest to Cormac fared the best, but as I trailed behind him, my sleeve was ripped off as they tried to grab me. Cormac yanked me through their ranks at a speed that would've done a track star proud.

We cleared the group ahead but they simply joined the mob behind us and there was nothing but a cliff wall in front of us as we ran.

"You need to open a portal. I can't float us up quick enough."

"Here?" I was in a complete state of panic.

"Yes, now. Before they start shooting at us."

"I don't know…"

"NOW."

I didn't know where it would lead but I prayed it would be somewhere on Earth. I used my free hand to try to direct the energy I was building from the surrounding area, having no idea how the hell I was going to pull it off, when I realized the entire cliff wall was ebony. Duh. I concentrated as hard as I could and it sprung open. We ran through it less than a second later.

We didn't stop once we were in it, either. We needed to get it shut down before they could follow us through. Not even paying attention to where we landed, I tumbled onto carpet, getting a nice case of rug burn before I finally collapsed. I took a deep breath and was relieved that I could. So grateful that the place we ended up had breathable air, it took me a second to realize I wasn't resting my head on just any red and gold carpet. I looked at the ground and knew I recognized the pattern. I raised my head to see the entire gaming floor of The Lacard Casino gaping at us, open mouthed. I scanned the perimeter and saw that we hadn't done too much damage. A couple of overturned gaming tables but no one was on the floor except for me.

"Thank you ladies and gentleman for partaking in the demo of our new and upcoming show - Magic." I turned to see Cormac already on his feet speaking to the crowd. "It will be premiering next month." He walked over and offered me a hand up, then turned back to the crowd. "Don't mind my assistant, she's a little wet behind the ears." The crowd let out a laugh as the tension broke.

I bent down, grabbed the bag with the book and left him on the floor to finish up since he was doing so well.

"My place," he said as he grabbed my arm and pulled me with him to his elevator.

"Why not my place?"

"I don't have the time or patience for this game right now. You can come with me or stay behind."

"I've got the book," I said as I dangled it in front of me.

"And I could take it from you in less than a second." He stepped into his private elevator and held the door open.

I knew he'd put up a fight if I took off to my place, which technically was still in his place. I was also pretty sure he'd win. It was so freaking annoying. I ground my teeth together as I stepped in after him.

"I thought we were supposed to be partners?" Both of us watched the floors and tick by while I waited for an answer.

"We are," he finally said.

"Then why do you keep getting to make all the calls?"

He looked down at me with a smirk. "Because, I'm the *senior* partner."

I looked back at him. "One of these days, I'm going to be strong enough to kick your ass."

"You'll get strong, but I wouldn't hold your breath for the day you'll be able to take me. Baby, I've got skills you can't even imagine," he said and the look in his eyes sent a chill through me.

And just like that, I couldn't look at him. It seemed like lately everything sounded sexual. Part of me wanted to call him out on it, but what if it was just in my head? Nope, the idea of him not having any clue on what I was even calling him out on was way too humiliating. It wasn't like he was trying to come on to me at all. What if my subconscious had some weird crush on him and it was all in my head? No. Not saying a word.

"How did you do that back there? Like you were wearing a shield or something," I asked diverting the subject.

"Everything has an electromagnetic field that repels or attracts, just like magnets do. I just amped mine up for a couple of minutes. I can extend it further when I'm attached to someone but only a certain distance."

I stared down at my hand, wondering if I could do it too.

The elevator doors slid open and we found Buzz, Ben and Dodd already waiting inside the penthouse. All playfulness left Cormac's expression the moment we stepped into the room.

"Get Vitor. Tell him he needs to get over here ASAP," he told Buzz and then turned to Ben. "Go down to Kever. Tell him to put all portals on lock down. No transporting until further notice."

Only Cormac, Dodd and I were left in the room when he dropped the bag, that held the single book we had managed to get from the wolves, on the table. "I hope it's worth it."

"What is it?" Dodd asked Cormac.

"I have no idea but we just pissed off a whole lot of wolves."

"Scary looking wolves," I added.

It might have been misplaced nervous energy but laughter that I couldn't seem to stop startled to bubble up in me. Cormac soon started to laugh as well as we stared at the book we'd just stolen, that we couldn't touch, read, and had no idea if it would even help.

I laughed even harder when Dodd let out a scream as he tried to touch it.

"What's wrong with you two? You couldn't give me a heads up on that one?" he said as he shook his hand trying to alleviate the pain.

I pulled out a chair, stared at the book and thought about what Cormac had just said. I hoped this book was worth it. My eyes fixated on it, I barely registered the sound of two chairs sliding against the floor as Dodd and Cormac joined me.

The three of us just sat there, trying to figure out a good way to approach it. Cormac stood and grabbed a pair of tongs from the wet bar, but when he tried to open the cover with them, he dropped them quickly and shook his hand.

I tried next with a long spoon I found, but barely even lifted the cover before the pain became overwhelming. We could touch it with other instruments, but opening it was turning out to be impossible.

"This is stupid." Dodd said after a few more minutes passed. "I'm just going to open the freaking thing. If I get stuck on it, just push me off like they do with people getting electrocuted." He reached over again and put his hand on it. He got it open all of an eighth of an inch before he crumpled to the ground.

"That bad?" I asked as I saw the cold sweat on his brow.

"Worse than when you shot me in the knee." His breathing was labored and he still gripped his arm.

"It's got to be something worth reading if they went through all of this to protect it," I said.

"Not necessarily," Cormac replied, as Dodd still lay on the ground.

Cormac and I turned as we heard Buzz and Vitor walk in the room. Vitor strolled in and walked directly to the book, giving me a small smile in greeting and pretty much ignoring everyone else.

"So what exactly happened?" he asked no one

in particular. Cormac relayed the details of how we got the book.

"This is getting quite sticky," Vitor replied after hearing the entire story.

"Really, I'm so glad you came over here to offer us such wisdom," Cormac said.

A look passed between them and all I could think was oh God, not this again.

"I'm shutting down the portal for now," Cormac threw out at him in a *what are you going to do about it* tone.

"You can't shut it down. We've got a contract."

That might have worked with Cormac a few months ago, but something had been changing in him lately. I didn't know what was bringing on the transformation but I'd sensed his disregard for the agreements he used to spend his life protecting and upholding. This confirmed what I'd suspected. I just didn't know what had caused the change.

"Which you and I are going to break," Cormac replied as he stepped into Vitor's personal space.

I looked to Dodd and Buzz, hoping they would try to calm the situation down, to see that all they were doing was moving in to position to watch Cormac's back. Goddamn men for you.

"And what about the wolves? It's their contract too. You just going to shut them out?"

Shit. Vitor, why can't you just stand down, I thought to myself. I swear, once you pick up that cape you just can't seem to get rid of the thing. It's like a bad holiday sweater and everyone wants to know why you aren't wearing the hideous thing. Because it's ugly, that's why! That's how I felt about my new 'good person' role. I was sick of wearing it. Why? Because it sucked. I longed for the days when I didn't care about anyone or anything. I would have just gone and sat out of range of the blows and maybe even gotten a snack for the show.

"Don't act like the wolves have any say in this. I've felt the magic that binds that contract. There isn't a single iota of wolf signature on that. Now, we are ending this contract tonight."

I watched as the vein in Cormac's neck pulsed and the quicker it throbbed, the more I lost hope that this would be resolved peacefully.

"That might be, but they still have a say," Vitor replied, standing nose to nose with Cormac.

You dumb, stupid Fae. Yep, that was my cue. I wasn't sure why, but the idea of Vitor getting pounded into submission still made me feel bad, even if he was a bit of a selfish jerk.

I stepped up to them and placed a hand on each of their chests, trying to nudge them apart.

"Stay out of this, Jo. I don't want you to get hurt," Vitor said.

"She can get as involved as she wants to. She's not the one that's going to get hurt."

I looked up into Cormac's eyes and saw something had snapped. We had now hit def con five.

"Vitor, if we open up that portal, there is going to be a swarm of angry wolves headed right for us." I waited a second then added, "Coming for me," just to make sure it was beyond question. I wasn't sure Cormac's death would weigh on his conscience much.

When he took a step back, I knew I was starting to make some headway.

"What of my people?" he asked Cormac. "You shut the portal, but I still have family there."

"Well? Is there something we can do about that?" I asked Cormac. In my head, I was wondering when I had become the most mature person in the room. Things really were spiraling out of control now. "Cormac, there must be some compromise here. I mean, Vitor is the one that got us the information on where to look."

"Yes. And he also almost got us killed," he replied. The accusation was there, but it lacked heat; I wasn't too concerned.

"I want my sister brought over and permanent residency for fifty more when it's reopened." Vitor, seeing his opportunity to gain now, slipped into business negotiator mode and tried to seize the opportunity.

I watched Cormac ponder over the terms. "You agree to destroy the current contract and it's a deal."

Vitor nodded.

Cormac nodded.

I sighed in relief. I had enough going on with a crazy Senator that was killing people and wolves now wanting us dead. I didn't need another battle to fight.

"Tomorrow, at midnight. My place," Vitor said, and Cormac nodded.

"Why then?" I asked, as no one else seemed to be finding the timing unusual.

Cormac turned to me to explain, "There are certain times during the day when magic is weaker.

It depends on what type of magic it is exactly, but midnight is usually the best bet. It's the time between two days that allows for a weakness in the contract. Certain days of the year make it easier but we don't have that kind of time."

Vitor left pretty quickly after it was arranged, not wanting to stay in Cormac's domain.

Cormac followed him out to go down and confirm that everyone that could run the portal knew it was shut down, but I stopped him before he left. "What if you can't break the contract?"

"We have to. This is much bigger than the wolves. We don't know where the senator comes from or where he gets his strength. We've got to keep this contained as much as we can. He's not human, which means he might come from there. We can't let in anyone that might aid him."

I thought back to how he was helping Tracker set up other wormholes. "And he wants them open, which means we don't," I added.

"Exactly."

I watched him go and I headed toward the guest suite, my old rooms. wanting a shower but also not wanting to be far from the book.

My hands shook as I turned on the water and let it flow over me, but I couldn't even enjoy that. Finishing up quickly, I asked Ben to get me a pair of Cormac's sweats and t-shirt. I was swimming in them but at least they were clean. Then I went and sat with the guys as everyone took their turn trying to get the book open.

When I got there, I found the doctor, Sabrina, there as well as Kever and another petite brunette

Keeper named Lucy, who I'd seen operate the portal.

There were others but I also knew the amount of people that Cormac really trusted was small, even among The Keepers.

Dodd had control of the remote as usual, but it didn't matter since I couldn't pay attention to the TV anyway. I just sat there, half in a trance, replaying Rick's image in my head, only occasionally startled as someone would try to open the book again and inevitably screamed out in pain.

At that moment, I didn't think things could get much worse. It felt much later than it was, since it had been the middle of the night on their planet, but here the eleven o'clock news was just coming on.

When I looked at the screen, I was shocked. They were older but I would have recognized them anywhere. After all, I'd thought that they were going to be my parents. How could I forget them? And now their pictures were on the TV.

The news reporter explained the chilling details of how Charles shot Maxine in the middle of a park. Then shot himself.

I thought I heard Dodd in the background, saying something about all the crazies out there now, but I was hypnotized by the TV.

It couldn't be. He'd just gone crazy. He hadn't seemed crazy when I was a child, because I was too young to notice. And what kind of judge was I anyway? I had a couple screws loose myself.

I would have been able to rationalize it away. I'd almost been there, if they had just not interviewed someone in the park. It was a woman in her early thirties describing her eyewitness account. Nothing more shocking than you would expect, considering what had just happened, until she told the reporter that he had spoken right before he blew his head off.

"What?" the reporter asked her.

Please, please, don't be what I think it's going to be, was all that ran through my mind as the witness rambled on about how strange it all seemed, but still not saying what he said. I pulled my knees up to my chest and half hid my face, as if I'd somehow be able to shield myself from the horrible truth I was afraid I was about to find out. Finally she said, "He said 'the senator says hello'. It was the strangest thing."

I closed my eyes and rested my forehead on my knees, frozen and immobilized, as my reality became a living nightmare. I didn't cry or scream. I did nothing. Some logical part of me reasoned that I was in shock.

Why me? I know people ask that all the time when bad things happen. I also thought I was done with that question and accepted life for whatever it handed me. It hadn't been all sweet and perfect but I'd gotten some good things too. When the senator had talked about payback that night, I hadn't thought it would come like this. My pain I could handle. This? No. I knew me and I knew my soft spots. I couldn't hold up under too much more of this. Just not the way I was built.

The door in the hallway shut and we all turned to see Cormac strut into the room.

"Any progress?" he asked and tilted his head in

the direction of the book, still sat on the table.

Dodd rattled off a list of our futile attempts but when I looked over at the two of them, Cormac only seemed to be paying half attention, his eyes glued on me. He made a not so subtle gesture of telling them we're through for the night and ushered everyone out. I fell in with everyone, as they headed through the door.

I'd put one foot into the hallway when Cormac's voice called from behind me, "Jo, wait up a minute."

Shit. I knew what I had to do and didn't want to discuss it with him. I hesitated for a few seconds then forced myself to turn around. Act natural.

"What's up?"

He walked over with purpose to where I still hovered in the doorway. His predatory nature was sometimes overwhelming and if it had been even a month ago, I would have run away screaming. We had a dark past, the two of us, but I didn't think he'd hurt me. Sometimes I thought I saw something else lingering in those predatory eyes that gave me a chill. But it was of a completely different nature and promised a whole different kind of hurt.

"Come in here."

I sauntered back in as if nothing were amiss other than what he already knew. I watched him close the door and then stand in front of it.

"You're acting weird."

"No I'm not."

"Yes, you are, and you aren't leaving until you tell me what's up."

"Cormac, we were just almost killed by a pack

of human wolves, ran through a wormhole to be dumped onto the casino floor in front of an audience. How normal could I be right now?" I watched his face, waiting to see if he was going to buy my story, but he was so damn hard to read sometimes. I saw a twitch in his left cheek but that could mean I was fine or maybe the guy was hungry. He was pretty solid, I imagined he had to eat a lot.

"I think you should stay here. I don't feel comfortable, with everything going on."

Nope, that wasn't good. It would be a lot harder to do anything under the Cormac microscope. As it was, I was going to have to figure a new way out of the garage.

"So, is everybody going to be staying here?"

"This is different."

"Why?"

Now his muscle definitely was twitching. "It just is."

"We are supposed to be partners, correct?" I didn't wait for an answer and he didn't give one. "It's bad enough you moved my trailer to your garage, but that's where I'm staying." And now came the big test. He stood like a statue in front of the door as I squeezed around him. He didn't move, but he didn't stop me either.

CHAPTER SEVEN

It was nine o'clock in the morning when I stood and stared at the building that housed the senator's office. That morning it had been tougher than ever to get out without a tail. I'd made it all the way down the car ramp to find a guy sitting at the bottom, drinking coffee and reading a paper in a lounge chair. No one ever tried to stop me from going anywhere, but didn't anybody realize a girl needs some privacy sometimes?

I'd turned around, made my way back in and headed to the main kitchen area where they received deliveries. I got a couple of strange looks from the kitchen staff but no goons followed.

Now, here I stood, a knife in one pocket and a gun in the other. Even if I couldn't kill him, maybe if he killed me he would stop trying to murder everyone I knew. Yes, that was me, always the optimist.

My hands were in my pockets so no one could

see I was shaking like a leaf. I strolled up to the front reception desk, dressed in my black pants suit, trying to act the part of someone politically involved. Someone who should've been here.

"I'm here to see the senator," I said as I approached the blond receptionist who looked even younger than I did.

"What's your name, Miss?"

"Josephine Davids." Why bother to lie? There were at least four cameras aimed at me anyway.

"Do you have an appointment?"

"No, but the senator knows me well."

That seemed to catch her attention and I realized the word 'well' might have given her the wrong impression.

"If you could just take a seat, I'll see if he can see you."

The chill in her voice confirmed she now thought I was a call girl. If this kept happening, I might need to get cards made up.

The upholstered chairs in the waiting area were quite comfortable for what it was worth. I watched the receptionist make a call and then greet another man that walked past and through the door that would lead to where I needed to go.

It wasn't long before a different man walked out through the same door. I saw his eyes scan the waiting area and lock on me, but he didn't approach. Blood pumped through my veins so hard and fast it dulled my hearing. Game on, I thought to myself.

Then he handed a white envelope to the receptionist and left. The receptionist stood and walked over to me with a forced smile on her face.

"The senator asked me to deliver this to you and apologizes but his schedule is too busy to see you today."

I accepted the envelope as I sat there befuddled. He wouldn't see me? We were arch enemies. This isn't how it happened in the movies. Where was our big confrontation? I get a card? I felt kind of cheated, to be honest.

Looking down at the sealed envelope in my hands, I counted her retreating footsteps, gauging her distance before I tore the seal open.

It was so nice of you to visit me today, but you'll need to reschedule.
The debt must be paid.

I was lost. I couldn't figure out the Senator's angle. Was this a personal vendetta but why go through all, this? Just kill me already. I sure couldn't figure out how this had anything to do with taking over the world. Then there were the wormholes we knew he was behind. What did they have to do with anything? My head spun with all the variables, nothing fitting neatly together like I thought it should.

I shoved the note in my pocket, half crumbling it as I did. All decorum was gone as I raced from the building, not caring what I looked like anymore. It was either that or storm the door that led to him. In my current mood, I'd end up killing innocent people in my efforts before I died a bloody death.

The second I got outside, I pulled the jacket off and undid another button of my blouse. The heat of

Vegas felt oppressive as I walked away from the showdown that hadn't happen. How silly I'd been to think I'd be able to end it today. After all, when did things ever work according to plan?

I stumbled blindly away from the building in search of space. When I finally stopped to look at where I was walking, I saw Cormac waiting by the curb. The crossed arms and look in his eyes told me there would be a showdown after all, just with a different adversary.

When I had anticipated this moment in my head, either the senator or I was supposed to be dead. If it was dead, then I'd have nothing to really worry about with Cormac. If I made it, how could anybody be pissed at the person that killed the bad guy?

He stood there in front of his newest Ferrari, which happened to be white. I didn't bother ignoring him, I had my own pent up anger and if he wanted a fight, so be it. I'd give him one.

"What?" Some words in life are very versatile. *What* could have sounded defensive, shocked or nonchalant. The way I just said it was more along the lines of *What* the fuck is your problem? This was definitely a cursing *what*.

He opened the car door and trumped my *what*, with his *in*. I was silently impressed with the amount of anger he was able to infuse into *in*. Yes, quite impressive.

Neither of us said anything on the way back to the casino. Nothing on the way upstairs either. When we walked into his penthouse, Dodd was there with Ben, but one look at us and they left without saying a word.

I heard the door shut and I counted off in my head, one Mississippi, two Mississippi...

"What the hell did you just do?"

I relayed a short account of what had occurred, seeing no reason to lie about it at this point and threw the senator's note on the table, for him to look at or not. Just when I thought he was going to be fairly calm, he blew.

"What the hell do you think you were doing!"

And there it was. He started pacing the room. Cormac has two types of paces: one type was the 'let me release some anger,' the other was 'I might kill someone.' They looked similar to the novice, but I'd started to determine the difference by the speed and heaviness of his step. We were definitely teetering into the latter variety.

"I was handling things," I replied, perhaps too calmly because my attitude seemed to be aggravating him more by the second. I'd never seen a third upgraded version of his pacing and I was slightly curious. Would he start to float in between steps or something equally as interesting?

"You think this is a joke?"

"Of course not."

"Did you just roll your eyes at me?"

"You have to admit, that was a dumb question."

Uh oh. He stopped pacing. I hadn't factored in him not having a third speed. He stood deathly still, all energy focused on me intently. Too intently.

"Do you want to die? Is that your deal?"

"No, that's a stupid thing to even say."

"Then why would you go there with no plan, no

backup and no idea how to even kill him?"

"When did I become so important? You shut down the portal; you don't need me anymore anyway."

"I just don't get you. There are billions of people on this Earth, all dying to be special. You are, and I watch you run from it every day. If that wasn't bad enough, now you practically throw away your life like it's nothing."

I thought I was ready for a fight, even itching for one, but now I just wanted to leave. "You know nothing about me and I don't have to sit here and listen to your bull!" Slamming the door behind me, I left his penthouse. I should have realized then that he'd let the fight go too easily, but I wasn't thinking that clearly.

His men followed me all the way to the garage but I didn't care. They could follow me to Hell if they wanted, as long as they stayed out of my way.

The minute I stepped into the garage a rage I didn't even think I was capable of consumed me. My trailer was gone.

I swung on the two goons that had followed me. "Where. Is. My. Trailer?" If I could have blown steam through my nose, I would've.

The two of them just shook their heads, looking baffled. I broke into a run, heading right back to the only person that would've messed with my stuff. It took me less than a minute to barge back into his penthouse, and only that long because the elevator could only climb so fast.

He was sitting on the couch, reclined and waiting.

"Where is my trailer?"

"It's in a safe location."

"Where?!"

"I'm not ready to divulge that information."

My whole body was shaking with rage as I stood over him where he sat. "You better tell me where it is."

"Or what?"

I lunged for him, prepared to inflict as much bodily harm as necessary to find out where my trailer was being hidden. My fists swung and connected but my glory was short lived as I found myself on my back with Cormac lying full on top of me, pressing me into the couch.

"I want my trailer back," I demanded, as if I still had leverage.

"I tried to do this the nice way. I tried to be partners. Unfortunately, you have issues working as a team and seem to need some incentive." He settled in a little closer and I started to wonder what incentive he meant. "So, your trailer will be held in an undisclosed location until I feel comfortable about your participation level."

"This is complete bullshit."

"Yes, that is exactly how I felt this morning when I was trying to track you all over town, to find that you had gone to find the senator."

"This is unacceptable and I won't tolerate it."

"Really? What do you plan on doing?"

Well, this was humiliating. I couldn't even get him to let me off the couch. What kind of brilliant threat did I pose? Lacking any adult response, I turned my head and refused to speak.

Then he shocked me. He kissed my cheek, ruffled my hair and stood, telling me he had ordered me a turkey club for lunch.

"You need serious meds. I really think you might be bipolar."

He paused at the door where I thought he was going to argue with me some more. "I had your clothes and things moved back as well. Hope you don't mind." Then he smiled, because I obviously did, and the bastard strolled from the room.

CHAPTER EIGHT

"We need to get a wolf," Buzz said.

"I told you, they won't cooperate," Cormac said.

"No, I mean a real wolf."

Cormac, Dodd, Ben, Dr. Sabrina, Kever and I all stared at him as we stood around the book in Cormac's penthouse.

"It's magically spelled somehow, but maybe if we used a real wolf, took his paw and used that to open it, it just might work."

It was either completely ridiculous or the most brilliant thing Buzz had ever said.

"But I thought they aren't really wolves? Aren't they just weird, mutating aliens?" I looked around, waiting for anyone other than Cormac to answer what I thought was a simple question.

Of course, Cormac was the one that did answer. "They are and they aren't. We've done some tissue sampling from them. We don't know how, but there is some sort of DNA link there." He turned toward Buzz. "Okay, big guy, you're up. Find us a wolf." We all stared at Buzz; I assumed everyone was thinking the same thing I was, why hadn't someone else in the room with a slightly higher IQ thought of it?

We watched as Buzz left the room, full of excitement over his idea, and Dodd sidled up next to me.

"What's up with you two?"

"Nothing."

"It's not nothing. You won't even look at him."

"I took her trailer," Cormac said, having come up behind us.

Dodd didn't speak, just made an 'oh' shape with his mouth and looked up at the ceiling.

I crossed my arms, refraining from clawing at Cormac's face.

"What happened?" Ben asked as he walked over and stood next to us.

I was still pissed off and having everyone here know he took my trailer made it all the worse. It was humiliating having my trailer stolen.

"Cormac stole her trailer," Dodd said in a hushed tone.

"Dodd, I'm not deaf. What is the point of whispering to Ben if I'm standing closer to him than you are?"

"Hey, I was just trying to be sensitive. Don't yell at me. I'm not the one that stole your trailer."

"I didn't steal her trailer. I simply took it for a while."

"Boss, why'd you steal her trailer?" Ben asked.

"I took her trailer because she needs to learn to work with others."

Dodd simply shook his head, disagreeing without words.

"Why do you think he took it then?" Ben asked.

"I can't disclose, but it wasn't the nicest way to go about getting it."

"Do you have something to say?" Cormac questioned Dodd.

"Nope, not saying another word." Dodd turned back to me, "Any word on Hammond?"

"No. I think he's lying under a mountain of rubble right now," I told Dodd. I wasn't sure how I felt about it either. I'd never known him and wasn't sure if I would've wanted to, but it might have been nice to have had the opportunity. It didn't matter now anyway. Even if he was alive, he would only be another target for the senator.

I looked around the room and realized every single person in there had a target on their back because of me. And there wasn't a single thing I could do about it.

"What about the portals? Are they all shut down?" I asked, directing my question at Dodd.

"Yep, everything. He's breaking the contract tonight," Dodd said, motioning toward Cormac, who now stood across the room.

"I don't get it. Is it magic or science? As soon as I think I've got my brain around how something works, I'm stumped by something else."

"Magic or science…sometimes I'm not sure there is a difference. Maybe magic is simply something that hasn't been scientifically explained yet."

I looked at the man I viewed as a carefree gigolo most of the time and I realized, like most people, there was a lot more under the top layer than he showed.

"I think I like the idea of magic. It's romantic somehow. I'm not sure I want everything to have an explanation."

"You are such a *girl*." And just as quick as that, the gigolo façade was firmly back in place. "I wouldn't worry about it if that's what you want, because unless that book on the table has thousands of years of our history, you aren't getting too many explanations."

I looked back at the book with the one inch thick binder. Nah, not likely. I wasn't going to complain though. Right now any information was better than what we had. If we could just open the damn thing. The most anyone had been able to do was move it; opening it had proved impossible.

Cormac was standing over it right now answering his phone while he stared at it. I could see the lust for knowledge in his eyes.

"You going to forgive him?" Dodd asked.

"I don't know."

"He almost died for you the other night."

"I'm sure he knew he'd be fine."

"No, I don't think he did. Snipers have taken out more of us than all other things combined. We can only take on so much damage before we shut down. We aren't invincible."

"I know that."

"So when you pranced into the senator's office,

you knew what could have happened?"

"I had my reasons."

"Yeah, reasons. You are one fucked up chick."

Before I could reply, I was distracted by Buzz walking into the living room with the ugliest, rattiest dog I'd ever seen. It looked like he had just come from a crazy groomer that didn't know how to handle an electric razor. If the hair wasn't matted, it was bald.

"What is that?" Kever asked.

"This is Abby," Buzz replied, holding onto the wolf's leash. It was the canine equivalent of the Charlie Brown Christmas tree. "I got her from Sue over at the Vegas Zoo. She's very docile but they don't like to let her run in the yard because of her hair disorder. She gets sunburned."

I was thinking it was more along the lines of they were embarrassed of her - I'd want a refund if I had paid to see this wolf.

"Ugh, she smells!" Ben chimed in. "Are you going to give her a bath?"

Abby was also quite intelligent, if not as docile as Buzz claimed, because at the mention of that word she raised her lip and growled at Ben.

"Let her off the leash," Cormac said. I wasn't sure if that was a great idea or not, but Buzz did it without hesitation. Cormac made a clicking noise and Abby trotted right over to him, tongue practically hitting the floor, and gave him the sloppiest lick I'd ever seen. Even the God damn dog? Was there no female immune to him? No wonder his ego was out of control.

"You're a smart girl, aren't you?" Cormac spoke

to the raggedy looking wolf and darned if she didn't yelp back in reply.

Even for a small wolf, she was a decent sized animal. When Cormac tapped the table, she jumped up and put her two front paws on it. He took one of her paws in his hand, which she licked again, and moved it toward the book.

"Wait," I yelled, stopping him. "Is that going to hurt her?"

"I'm only going to brush her near it. I'm not going to hold her paw there."

I cringed but nodded. I watched as he took her paw and glanced the book with it. Nothing. No yelps of pain, Abby was completely unfazed. Next, he took her paw and lifted the front cover. Again, all was fine.

"And we're in," he said as the cover thudded onto the table, making a much louder noise than something that weighed less than a pound should've.

We all rushed in closer and crowded around the table. I inadvertently ended up squeezing next to Cormac, and I swear Abby gave me the evil eye. Which I, of course, returned.

I looked down at the title page that read gibberish, gibberish, blah blah…KEEPERS.

"Can anybody here read this?"

"A couple of words, but I'm not going to make heads or tails of this," Dodd said and laughed over his own goofy joke.

"I'll stop by Burrom's on the way back from Vitor's and get someone there. It's getting late. I gotta be at Vitor's by midnight."

Cormac grabbed his keys and I ran and grabbed my purse.

He looked at me as I went to leave with him. "What are you doing?"

"I'm coming with you."

Dodd stepped over quickly. "Boss, you think that's a good idea? That place is crawling with wolves and they're pretty pissed off right now."

"Dodd, stay out of this. I'm going."

Cormac opened his mouth, and I saw the beginning of a 'no' form on his lips.

"Oh, I don't think so. I either go with you or I go and do my own investigating. Your choice." I stood, hands on hips, daring him to say no now.

"Fine."

"Do you want me to come with?" Dodd asked.

"No, stay and try to figure out as much as you can until I get back."

I could see he was uneasy about taking me but I didn't care. If he took my trailer for cooperation then I better get full access to stuff to cooperate on.

It took a while for us to get over to Vitor's, and when we got there, we were the only visitors. We walked into the place like we owned it to find Vitor lounged on his couch in the great room. When he turned to see us, I thought I saw a twinkle of surprise when I stepped out from behind Cormac.

"Are you ready?" he asked as he stood and walked toward us, dressed elegantly in dark grey slacks and a linen shirt.

Neither of us replied. Me? I thought it was pretty obvious since we were standing in his house. I have no idea why Cormac ignored him. No, actually, I think I do.

"I'm surprised you brought Jo. It's a little dangerous, isn't it?"

"He brought Jo because she makes her own decisions, and she is also not a precious creampuff that will deflate," I told him.

"Okay then. Follow me."

He walked out the glass doors at the back of the house as we followed him out. We didn't stop outside but kept going about another five hundred feet, to where a circle of candles stood. There had to be about a hundred of them, all blazing a little stronger than was natural.

"We need to open up access to the other planes of existence to do this. The magic that binds the contracts is leaked into this plane from the others that we can't normally see."

I looked around, feeling like I should be able to see something that existed all around us. "So, there is another plane of existence right here, right now?"

"Yes, and that is where all magic stems from."

"You can't step out of this circle while we are canceling the contract," Cormac said, as we stepped into the center. "In this circle, we will penetrate some of the boundaries that keep the different planes separated."

"Where is the contract?" Looking at the both of them, I figured it would be here.

"We don't have it." Vitor answered.

"I don't know much, but wouldn't that make it harder?"

"Yes. A lot." Cormac's voice told me more than his words. This was going to be a heavy scene.

"Stay close."

That didn't sound good. "What should I do? I mean, other than possibly running."

To Cormac's credit, he still smiled at my bad joke even though he was tense.

He held his hand out to me. "We could use the extra juice, now that you've offered."

"You two ready?" Vitor asked.

Both Cormac and I nodded. Then he tugged my hand to get my attention. "Don't get freaked out if you see anything…odd. It can't touch us."

"What would I be seeing?"

"It's usually just a haze, nothing too freaky."

"What exactly is going to happen?"

Vitor answered as he stepped closer to us. "Since we don't have the physical contract, we have to reach out and try to find its energy thread. All energy has a trail and all spells are connected here, and in the other planes of existence, by a link. Think of it like an umbilical cord of sorts. The other planes feed the magic to this side. We just have to find it."

"Why does that sound sort of iffy?" I looked at the two of them and neither instilled any real sense of confidence in me. "I know The Keepers were crap historians, but what about your people, Vitor? Did they leave you any idea how to locate this connection?"

"You mean the people that are about to get the shaft and be completely shut off from Earth?"

"Yeah, those people. I'm sure they'd want to pitch in," I said in a mocking tone, feeling ridiculous that I hadn't thought that one out better.

Cormac looked at his watch. "Eleven fifty-nine. Let's get this going before it's that much harder."

I nodded and Vitor started to count down. When he hit one, they both started chanting in a language I didn't understand. At least I thought it was a language. I could feel the air become charged with energy. Just like when I was going to a new planet, I felt exhilaration wash over me. Hmmm, maybe it isn't a hero trait. Am I becoming an adrenaline junky?

I looked upward as the sky shimmered and the stars looked a little brighter, and the candles started to burn more intensely. As I looked upward again, I saw tendrils of silver smoke start to snake along above us. Vitor raised his hands and they moved as his did, not touching, but parallel to his motions; it was a mesmerizing dance that I could've watched all night.

It seemed a gentle give and take, as he probed and played with the ribbon and the strands became more abundant, creating a marble swirl of sky above us.

"I've got it," Vitor said, his hands stilling. Cormac stepped closer to him, beneath the strand he had indicated and raised his right hand, still holding my hand in his left.

I didn't know exactly how they did it, but that one strand started to dissipate into the sky, until it left a clear spot where it had been.

"Do you think that's it?" Cormac asked Vitor.

"I think so," he replied, still swirling his hand around the haze. "I don't feel anything else, do you?"

"No. Let's shut it down then." Just as Cormac said that, he lowered his arm and several of the swirls followed lower than any of them had dipped before. "What's going on? Did you do something?" He turned accusingly toward Vitor.

"No, you've seen everything I've done."

"Hurry up. Shut it down." The swirls didn't touch Cormac at all, just traveled several inches away from his body, all the way down his left arm. Cormac instantly dropped my hand, not wanting them to get to me, but it was too late. They traveled the path between us.

"Don't worry. They can't touch you."

Don't worry? Swirls of an unknown entity were circling around me as he again yelled at Vitor to close it off. Vitor, equally panicked, screamed back that he was trying. Yeah, no worries. Sure.

The silver tendrils came closer and then glided along my skin.

Cormac came and started to swat them away.

"Wait. Stop. They aren't hurting me and I think you are making them angry."

"We don't know what they are doing."

"They're checking me out. Smelling me, almost like a dog would."

"How do you know that?"

"I'm not sure. It's just a feeling I have."

They swirled around and I forced myself to relax even as they circled around my neck. They did this for several minutes more, and then suddenly they floated up toward the rest of them as they all dissipated.

"What the hell was that?" Vitor said, not really

asking either of us.

"Probably just a fluke," Cormac answered.
"You want to draw up the new contract?"

"No, not tonight. I think we should give it a few
days."

Cormac agreed and Vitor couldn't have ushered
us off his land any quicker without being downright
rude, but I didn't care. I still felt a tingling over my
arms. Even though I was acting calm, it had startled
me and the quiet ride home soothed my nerves.

"You good with stopping at Burrom's? I can
drop you off first," Cormac said, disturbing the
perfect calm of the car. I'd always loved driving at
night. Just the interior lights on and soft music.

"No, I'm good." He didn't say anything else and
I leaned my head back and watched the stars
twinkle as we headed back to town. As we pulled
into the familiar alleyway, memories flooded back.
I wasn't sure now which was more disturbing,
seeing Cormac bleeding out onto the dirty
pavement, or my encounter with the senator.

We walked into Burrom's place, which was
even more crowded than last time. I was slightly
taken aback by all the new faces; all decidedly
angry looking. Faces I knew I hadn't helped come
over. Where were they all coming from, if I hadn't
brought them and we were shut down?

I turned to Cormac, a silent question in my
eyes. He gave me a single nod in acknowledgment.
Sometimes, in times like these, I found it odd how I
could find myself so in sync with someone so
different to me.

We moved toward Burrom, who sat in the exact

same place as the last time I had come here. It appeared that perhaps this was just the little man's spot, so to speak. As we navigated through the equivalent of an angry hornet's nest, temporarily lulled by smoke, I eyed up the angry beasts and tallied their numbers in my head.

It wasn't too long ago that I would've felt a bit overwhelmed by taking on more than two of them, but something had honed in me while I had worked the wormhole. I still had my issues and I seriously lacked control, but I felt it. 'It' being the raw, undiluted power that welled up in me the more I tapped into it. It made me heady. I wonder if that was what made the senator retreat from me that night. I didn't know what he was, but had he sensed it?

"Why should I speak with you?" were the words that greeted us when we reached Burrom.

"Not here," Cormac replied in a peremptory manner.

The little man folded quickly and we joined him in the back.

"Burrom, you know I had to do that," Cormac said, relenting a bit now that he had asserted his dominance.

"How am I supposed to keep this crew calm?"

"You don't have to. I'll handle anyone that gets out of line."

"Who are the new faces?" I asked, with an uncomfortable feeling.

"I don't know. There has been a steady stream of them lately. I thought you guys had ushered them in before the shut down."

"No," I replied, knowing the faces that had come over lately better than anyone else. The craziest part, and the thing that freaked me out the most, about what Burrom had just said wasn't the strange new faces. When had I become part of '*you guys*?' When had operating the wormhole occasionally morphed into a full time gig, morphed into being one of *you guys*? I was a one woman show.

"We need a translator. We have one of their books."

"That's a tough order."

"I know. I also know that you can get one. Price doesn't matter and you know the benefits working with us brings."

"It might take a while."

Cormac held the office door open for me as he turned back to Burrom. "Send them to my penthouse tomorrow at eight."

CHAPTER NINE

"How long have you been at it? Any progress?"
I asked Dodd as I walked into the living room in
Cormac's penthouse, where he sat with Abby beside
him. My temporary home until I located where he
had hidden my trailer. So far it wasn't going so well.
I hadn't managed to get anyone to leak even a hint
about its location.

"A little bit. You got someone coming tonight,
right?"

"In about twenty minutes. Why? What did you
find?" Something in his tone caught my attention.

"I might be wrong, so I don't want to say
anything."

"Dodd, you can't say something like *that* and
not say it."

"I'm just not sure I'm right. I only have a
rudimentary knowledge of this language, from some
girl I dated way back when. I don't want to freak
you out."

I grabbed a coffee and sat on the couch opposite him. "You've already scared me. Spill it."

"Abby," he said and pointed to the left side of the book. I watched the wolf take her paw and turn the page back.

"Wow, did you just teach her that?"

"She's quite smart." He leaned over the book page with a scowl.

"Just tell me, already."

"If I'm correct, it says something about a monster for good that was contained but not destroyed."

"Which is probably the senator. We already knew that. What's got you out of sorts?"

"If this book is correct and I'm reading it right, it says we created it and that it is indestructible." He took a long breath in between clenched teeth before he continued. "It might also say it's going to wreak havoc on the world, cause mass destruction, and kill a large portion of mankind."

At first I just sat there with my mouth gaping open. I sat there for probably a good minute, as Dodd just nodded his head in silent commiseration.

The next feeling I had was a desire to get up and run around the room screaming 'oh God, oh God, God.' Then I got a handle on my emotions. It was a book. Who the hell knew if the thing was even accurate and I said as much to Dodd.

"Yes, I agree. What makes me nervous is Cormac told me about the note that was left with the priest. The same thing is written in here."

"You mean the Golden Child Omen?" That was the name I'd given the omen that had been given to me by the priest.

"Yep. It's got an extra couple of lines but I can't figure out what they say. If it got those things right, how many more things are correct?"

"What do you think it says, if you had to guess?"

"We both know the first part, 'A golden child born and left will be the hope of those bereft. When eternal lilies bloom after a torturous night, the giver of gifts will stand for the right. The one who's sought is suddenly found, it will come time to stand their ground. So comes the reckoning where many fall. Tis not the end, but the start of it all.' But then, there are a couple more lines afterward. I can't understand most of it, but the end of the first sentence is 'all grown' and then all I can make out in the next sentence is 'throne'."

"Basically, you have no idea what it says?"

"Pretty much."

"It doesn't matter. It's wrong. Nothing is indestructible."

"I hope you're right." Dodd stood and stretched, as if his muscles were cramped. They probably were. He didn't look like the type to be hunched over a book for that long, but I was starting to suspect there might be a bit of nerd buried underneath all those muscles.

I sat on the soft leather sofa for a few minutes, letting my brain digest the possibilities. They were looking really bad; maybe even worse than I'd thought.

I'd tried to throw myself on the bomb to protect everyone. That hadn't worked out well. In bad times, your brain has a way of becoming crystal clear on priorities. There weren't many people I cared about, although the list was starting to get longer lately. The wall around me was showing cracks in the mortar. You know what happens when you try to fix cracks in cement? Shit. Give it a try, sometime. You think you're fixed - solid and as good as new. Then a chip appears and from there on out, it just keeps falling apart. It's a losing battle.

We both turned as we heard people entering the penthouse and Dodd looked at me and gave me a silent shake of his head. Cormac was already entering the room with a stranger, or I would have told Dodd not to sweat it; I'd never been fond of delivering bad news. Having an abundance of it to deliver hadn't changed my enthusiasm any.

"Dodd, Jo, this is Dark," Cormac said as he introduced the straggliest kid I'd ever seen. He looked like a cross between a skateboarder and a heroin addict; greasy light brown hair obscured half his face, hanging past his shoulders.

He flipped his hair and smiled with beautiful straight white teeth; he had the nicest skin I'd ever seen. "Hi. Sorry if my hair is a mess. I was in the middle of a deep conditioning treatment when I got the call."

"What's with the clothes?" Dodd asked, lacking tact as usual.

"Dude, I'm blending."

"With who? Meth heads?"

His face sank and I couldn't help but feel for

the kid. "Really?" Dark asked not masking his disappointment at all. He looked at me and Cormac, clearly hoping for a more approving second opinion.

"It's not that bad," I told him, mostly out of pity.

Dodd patted him on the back. "Don't worry about it kid. I'll help you out."

Cormac cleared his throat, commanding attention. "Later. Right now I need you to translate this book for us."

"This one, dude?"

"Yes, and it's Cormac."

The kid shrugged, letting the correction roll off his back. He grabbed the book with no problems, and sat down on the couch with it in his lap.

"How come you can touch it and we can't?" I asked.

"Just the way our stuff works. I don't know how, though."

Cormac, Dodd and I sat across from him on the couch, staring at him like he was the bearded woman at a side show freak exhibit.

I tried to be patient as we sat there but Cormac was tense, I could literally feel his agitation. Dodd was fidgeting like the energizer bunny, and I knew why, which added to my tension. The kid? Calm as a cucumber. Oh to be young and stupid again. I felt like I'd aged fifty years in these last months.

"Well?" I finally said, after watching him for about ten minutes. "Do you know what it says?"

"Of course. It's my language."

"What's it say?"

"A lot. It's going to take me a while to read it all but it seems to be a partial history, of a sort, about your kind."

"Sort of?"

"Yeah, the intro says it's written by one of my kind that was around during some heavy shit that happened with your kind."

Dodd finally exploded from his seat like the ticking time bomb he was becoming. "What does it say on the page that has an x type shape with two things that look like sixes near them?"

The kid flipped to the page Dodd asked about and I saw it on his face the moment he read the passage. Dodd was right.

"What is it?" Cormac asked, the only one left out of the loop.

"Okay, I'm going to read it but don't shoot the messenger, okay?"

"I'll shoot you if you don't read it right now."

"Fine," the kid said sulkily, but not showing any real fear. "The author writes that The Keepers created a beast of magnificent power. He knows that their intentions were good but that they were warned by many of his kind and the Fae folk to not dabble in these arts. That the great prophesier had seen our doom in it. That with this creation, they were sowing the inevitable death and destruction of both of our worlds."

"Did it say anything about indestructible?" I asked.

The kid scanned the page. "Oh, yeah. Sorry. I missed that part."

I leaned back, deflated. "I bet this is why the

older Keepers destroyed their history. They weren't paranoid. They were scared." I resisted the urge to start biting my fingernails. It wasn't a habit I'd ever had before, but I understood it now. "Dodd, what page was the prophecy on? I want to know what the two extra lines are."

Dodd walked over to him and Dark flipped through until Dodd found it. "There," he said as he pointed. "What are those lines saying?"

"For when the golden child is finally grown, she will help the beast claim his throne," Dark read.

No one said anything until the kid broke the silence. "Who's the kid? Do you know? Maybe you should take them out?"

"Shut up," Cormac said

"It's wrong." I didn't care if the first part of the omen was correct. The ending wasn't.

Cormac stood as well now. I had a feeling he was fighting off the same urge I had before. It was hard to look like a big bad tough guy though if you ran screaming around the room. Not to mention it would have freaked me out that much more, so I appreciated the restraint.

Cormac walked over and hovered next to the kid, making him appear even smaller and lankier than he was, and tried to read over his shoulder. He sighed and I recognized the frustration in his voice. I felt it myself. It came from feeling helpless. Inadequate.

He walked from the room but came right back and handed the kid a laptop. "Everything. Every word, period and comma if you guys have them. I want them all translated into a file in here."

"Nice hardware!" Dark exclaimed taking the computer from Cormac.

"Get it done quickly and it's yours."

"Awesome!"

"Dodd, hang out here with the kid. I'll be in my office if you need me." Then he looked at me. It was clearly a look that said *stay out of trouble*.

I rolled my eyes. *Yeah, yeah.*

As soon as he left, I got up and went to get into some trouble. Sometimes these things were inevitable.

CHAPTER TEN

I couldn't do anything about Cormac, Dodd or any of the other Keepers. Their fate was tied to mine, but I could do something about one person.

I grabbed my phone from the table, started to dial...and stopped. An image of the contract I'd signed jammed full force into my brain. Some pain or watching another person die for me? I'd choose the physical pain, that payback of a variety I could handle.

"Where've you been? I never got to hear about your date." Lacey wasn't an hello person, but she was a fragile human that would be one of the easiest targets around me.

"I don't have time to tell you about it now. Can you meet me in Cormac's garage?"

"At your trailer?"

"My trailer isn't there but it doesn't matter. I'll explain when you get here. I just need you to come now."

DONNA AUGUSTINE

"I have a mani pedi appointment but I'll come after that."

"No, you've got to come now."

"Can't. My nails are chipped and I've got a shift tonight. I refuse to be seen like this."

"Call out of your shift for tonight. I'll give you the money. You've got to come now."

"Where are you going to get the money? How much is that new position paying?"

"Lacey, please!"

"Okay! I'm coming now. I'll cancel work but I'm telling them it's your fault. I don't know how, exactly, but I'll think of something. Arnold is already pissed at me for calling out last week."

"I'll take the heat. Just come." I hung up before she could think of another reason and headed to the garage before she got there.

Looking around the garage, I saw a new mustang where my trailer used to be. With everything going on, it was amazing he still found time to shop.

True to her word, Lacey was in the garage five minutes later. Her manicurist was located in The Lacard mall, so it wasn't that impressive.

"What are you all weird about?" She huffed as she strolled in, clearly put out about her still chipped polish.

"You should probably sit down for this."

"Where? I'm standing in a garage. You are acting so odd lately," she said, then leaned against a vintage Rolls Royce, crossed her ankles and made an ugly face as she eyed her toe nails.

"I want you to take this, pack up your family,

128

and get out of Nevada." I handed her a large manila envelope that was bursting at the seams with my island down payment. Bye bye palm trees and cool tropical breezes, margaritas on the deck overlooking the ocean.

She looked at me skeptically. I knew she thought I was crazed by now.

"You've cracked completely. You've always been an odd bird, but you've totally lost it."

She took the envelope from my hand and opened it.

"Now I know you've lost it. You don't have this kind of money. I can't believe you're making me lose a shift for a joke. What are these, fake bills? You know it's illegal to make fake money."

"It's real. Take it to a bank, they'll confirm it. My life would be so much easier if you could just take my word on this. It's not safe here anymore."

"Why isn't it safe?"

I'd known this was too outlandish for any sane human to believe without some sort of proof, which meant I was screwed. I hoped there were some prescription drugs around here to take the edge off whatever was going to be heading my way. I didn't think ibuprofen was going to cut it.

"I'm going to tell you, but I don't know how much time I'll have after I do. No matter what happens, don't worry about me, I'll be fine. You just need to leave afterward. Agreed?"

"If it's really a problem and you aren't crazy, then yes, I'll leave."

"Cormac has a wormhole in the basement of this casino that I help to operate, using the power to convert the physics of normal matter into exotic matter. Aliens, that you would know as Werewolves and Fae, come in and out of this wormhole. There is another creature that is making people shoot themselves and possibly wants to take over the world. I don't know why, but he doesn't like me at all. He's killing people close to me. Also, there are strange werewolves showing up and they aren't friendly. The town is going down and it might start going down fast."

Her eyes were wide open and her jaw slack. Finally, she uttered a single "Huh?"

"I know you are going to want to see physical proof." I looked around for the first thing I could find and it was a random stone probably dragged in from a tire. I wrapped my hand around it for a minute and when I released it, it shot up toward the ceiling making a dent and stayed there.

"How did you do that?"

"I told you."

A shimmer glistened in the air like someone had taken a super fine sparkling dust and released it into a cyclone.

"What is that? Are you doing that too?" Lacey asked now in near hysteria.

"No, but I think you should get going." I didn't add that a whole lot of hurt was about to hit. I didn't know how these things worked and I didn't want to get her entangled. This was coming for me and I'd take it on my own.

"What did you do?" Cormac asked from the entrance. It was a rhetorical question. I could see from his face he already knew. Dodd was behind him as he strode into the large garage, and just shook his head while muttering something about god dam stupid girl and death wish.

"Get her out of here," Cormac said to Dodd as he pointed toward Lacey. "Make sure you tie up the loose ends."

Dodd grabbed Lacey by the arm and I went to lunge for the two of them but Cormac blocked me.

"What are you doing?" I screamed.

"Getting her out of here before she sees anything else and it goes beyond where I can fix things."

"How? By killing her?" I took a swing at him knowing it was a long shot but desperately trying to get past him to Lacey.

"No, the contract is already voided," he said as he blocked the punch. "I'm not going to kill her, but I might kill you." I watched him pull his phone out and dial. I didn't know who he was talking to but he relayed what had just happened without me telling him a thing. He grabbed me by the arm and pushed me into the Ferrari as he was still talking.

"I'm going to be in a whole lotta pain soon. I'm not sure this is the time for an outing." I started to get out of the seat but he pushed me back in.

"Stay."

"I'm not a dog."

I leaned back in the seat anyway deciding to let this play out if he was going to be so crazy about it.

He gripped the steering wheel so tight I was surprised it didn't break in two as we skidded out of the garage, cutting off traffic as we went.

"Once the pain starts, it might be a good idea to

head back." I wasn't sure if he was paying attention or not but I figured it couldn't hurt to give him a warning that this might be a short trip.

"You are going to be a whole lot of nothing soon if I don't get you some help."

"What exactly do you mean by nothing?"

"Dead. That's what I mean." He turned and threw me a look that iced the blood in my veins.

"Dead, like final death kinda dead?"

"What didn't you not understand about DON'T. TELL. HUMANS?"

"I had to."

"When have you ever *had* to do anything?"

The tires screeched as we pulled into the alley near Burrom's just as his words hit home. I've done some stupid things, I'd even went to confront the senator alone, when I knew he was a monster, but every other time I'd always had a fighting chance. What would this be like? I didn't even know what would come for me. And on a side note, was he really going to make me die here, at Burrom's? The place was stinky and dirty. That's just not right.

He grabbed my hand and pulled me after him when I hesitated by the door.

I tugged back. "I'm not dying in there. I'd rather kick it in the alley, if need be."

"You're not dying anywhere. Come on, we don't have a lot of time."

"You just told me I was? Am I dying or not?" I screamed at his back as we moved through the packed room playing Nine Inch Nails so loud I could barely hear.

"Not if I have anything to do with it," he said as

he kept moving forward. He released my hand and stepped up on the top of the stage in the back of the room. He made a hand gesture and the music immediately stopped. "I need every Fae here to follow me to the roof. If you want to live on my planet even one more day you'll do what I'm saying." He jumped off the stage and walked toward a staircase in the back where Burrom waited.

Cormac paused and looked at the room full of Fae that were still seated. "NOW," he said in a voice that echoed through the bar room, shattering glasses and a couple of the mirrors hanging.

"Hurry, we don't have much time," Burrom said as he eyed me up and down.

I heard the feet shuffling of the Fae as they all opted to do what Cormac asked before he showed them any more tricks he had.

In the dim light, I realized the strange shimmering was hovering around me. It had followed me from Cormac's garage. *Hello, Death*, I silently greeted it. *At least now you have a face.* Yep, that didn't make me feel much better at all.

I climbed the stairs with a mass of thirty Fae at my back, Cormac at my side and Burrom leading the way. My legs felt numb from panic and I wondered how I moved forward.

And just like that, it hit me. I'd always thought I would be cool with death. When it's your time, you go. Now that it was truly here, I realized I'd been an utter fool. I didn't want to go silently into the night, I wanted to kick the doors down and go out screaming and raging, clinging to every last breath.

"So, what are my odds? Do I have a shot?" I

asked Cormac as we still had a half a flight to go.

"Finally," he replied, "took you long enough."

"Not helping."

"You aren't going anywhere." There was steel in his voice when he said it and I hoped he was right.

"Put her in the center. Quickly!" Burrom said as the Fae circled around me.

Cormac, still standing next to me, grabbed me by the back of my hair and tilted my head back. His lips covered mine. 'No' didn't even enter my head. I didn't care about the past right now, I was a dying woman having a final moment, and oh what a moment it was. There had always been a lot of tension between us and it manifested itself there a thousand fold.

"Cormac, we don't have time!" It was Burrom's voice again and I just remembered we were standing in a circle of Fae, all witnessing this moment.

"Don't fucking die," Cormac said as he pulled back.

"God, you are such a romantic," I replied. He smiled but it was bittersweet and we both knew it.

Burrom looked to me. "We are going to try to buffer the force. The more we can absorb the better chance you have."

I nodded like I knew what he meant. Looking up, the shimmering had started to intensify. *No, I don't say hello to you. You can go fuck yourself, you shimmering shit!* I didn't say it aloud. If I was going to die, I preferred 'shimmering shit' not to be my last words.

The Fae chanted sounds I'd never heard as I stared at an enemy I could never have imagined. I'd come a hell of a long way in my life to die now. Abandoned to a foster care system, to living on the streets and mugging people to get by and some shimmering shit was going to take me out because I told a friend a couple of things to protect her. Was there even a God? Why hadn't I been killed when I'd robbed and stolen from innocents? I turned my life around and tried to do the right thing and now I'm going to die? What kind of bullshit rules were these?

The shimmering just intensified. So much so, I started to wonder if they weren't doing more harm than good. Maybe the Fae were trying to actually take me out. I eyed them with suspicion, now. No, Cormac wouldn't have brought me here if he thought there was even a chance they'd screw me. As strange as it seemed, I trusted Cormac. Never thought I would, but life is sometimes stranger than fiction. Looking at the sparkling reaper above my head proved it. I'd never imagine Death to look all sparkly, like a fifteen year old's eye shadow.

And then it began its slow creep toward me. And only me. From the way it was winding down, I'd say their chants were doing didley squat.

"Okay fairy dust, let's see what you've got. I've got a couple of tricks up my sleeve too."

The pain didn't come immediately. In a weird way, I almost felt as if it were playing with me. It was a slight tingle here and there. The kind you would get from a low charge battery. But it didn't stay that way for long. Soon, it began to feel like cigarette burns; I looked down as one touched my arm but it didn't leave a mark. Then it felt like cigar sized burns and those didn't come and go as quickly.

I felt the eyes of Cormac and the Fae on me and I tried to keep my dignity but with each moment I felt closer to the edge. By time it got to about fifty burns at once, all staying in place for almost a minute, I had to bite my cheek to keep from crying out.

My eyes were watering to a dangerous level, if I wanted to try and die like a true bad ass. I tried to breathe through the pain and realized that breathing through stuff is crap. The only good thing it might accomplish is passing out from hyperventilation. I started sucking wind. In these kinds of situations, I guess you take whatever you can get.

As the shimmering mist grew thicker around me, I saw Cormac break ranks as he tried to force his way in. It looked like he was trying to wade through hardening cement from where I watched. I was relieved, in one sense. I wasn't going to be able to hold it together much longer and the thick haze was starting to block out my vision of them and everything else around me, cocooning me in pain. At least I'd be dead when they saw me next and not writhing around in agony, begging for mercy.

But man, I'd been alone my whole life. I didn't want to die alone. If somehow I made it, I didn't want to live alone anymore either. Not being able to remain standing under the crushing pain, I fell to my knees, knowing no one would see my final defeat. I closed my eyes and tried to imagine the way the desert night sky looked when you got far away from the city lights. I should have told Cormac, I wanted to be buried out there somewhere.

A cool tingle around my ankle, in contrast to the burning, startled me. At first, I thought it was going to begin a new type of pain. It didn't. I looked down to find the same silver mist ribbon I had seen the night Cormac and Vitor had broken the contract.

And somehow, I sensed it wanted to help. I reached a few fingers out to it, not having the strength to lift my arm, and it grew in a long stream, slowly stretching and wrapping around them, similar to a toddler's grasp of your finger.

"Help me." I didn't know if it could, but I had a strong feeling it wanted to.

It weaved its way closer to my face and…nuzzled me? Yes, that was the only way it could be explained. It started to grow. I didn't know where the mass came from but it grew larger and larger as I watched, pushing back at the shimmering haze that was causing me so much pain. It pressed the haze back further and further. With each inch, the pain receded with it. Then it was gone. The shimmering haze, the white mist…both.

Cormac was there by my side less than a second later. When Cormac went to lift me, I gave him a look. We were on shaky ground with most of these Fae. This wasn't the time to show weakness. He backed off, but not all the way. He'd honor my request…to a degree. His hand on my elbow took more of my weight than one would imagine.

"What did you do?" Burrom asked.

The Fae all looked on me warily. Did I think

the Fae would turn on us? No, not really. Did they have ties with the wolves that would? One hundred percent. In this instance though, an exaggerated truth might serve better than a lie.

"I called for help."

"From who? There is no one here."

"No one you can see. I don't know what name you have for them, but I call them…" what the hell do I call them? Holy shit, come up with something cool quick before you look like a total fraud. "Magic Tethers. They are the silver ribbon strands that attach magic to this Earthly plane." Damn, I wish I could pat myself on the back because I was good! I saw a glint of humor in Cormac's eyes but other than that slight crinkle, he was pure stone.

"And how do you talk to them? How is that even possible?"

"I have no explanation. For me, it as if I were talking to you. No difference." I scanned the Fae, all clumped together near Burrom now, and saw in their faces, I'd risen in their estimation. I'd just done… well, I didn't know exactly what, but it was pretty damn cool.

"We've got to get back," Cormac said as he ushered me off the roof, not wanting to answer questions any more than I did about what just happened.

"You okay?" he asked softly as we headed down the stairs alone. The Fae had opted to stay on the roof, I'm sure to gossip about yours truly.

"I'm not dead," was all I said, all the relief I felt poured into those three words.

Now that I wasn't about to die, the anger I felt

from the wolves when we stepped into the main bar room was apparent and slightly overwhelming. It didn't seem to bother Cormac as he strode through the crowd with the arrogance of being untouchable, and no one tried to stop us as we left.

When we stepped outside, I realized we weren't out of the woods yet when I saw the group of approximately thirty wolves, who stood between us and Cormac's car. Uggh, didn't these people realize I'd already filled my almost getting killed quota for the day? No more shit, at least not until I got a good nap in.

I heard a rustle behind me and turned to see that all the wolves from inside had followed us out. No nap for me.

"This is not the time," Cormac said in a voice that would make any sane being run for the hills.

"This is exactly the time," the obvious leader of the group said. Nope, I guess not so sane. "I've heard some very disturbing things. Things that need to be answered."

Cormac looked to me, trying to gauge what I had left in me. I was starting to understand how Cormac thought. Appease the wolves for my sake or take them on because it's what he really wanted to do. I shrugged, effectively telling him to have at it. He didn't look convinced I had that much left in the tank.

"Answers you aren't going to get until I'm ready to give them. Now I'd step away from my car before I make you."

"Really? You think you arc that good?"

"I know I am."

And then they stared at each other like two men who didn't want to lose face but didn't want to fight either. Cormac wasn't scared of a fight. I wouldn't be surprised if he'd punched his mother's doctor on his way out of the womb. This other scraggly wolf guy? My senses told me he was bluffing. He was scared of Cormac. I couldn't even think poorly of him for it. If I were him, I'd be scared too.

But none of this helped my situation or got me to a bed any sooner, so I decided to take things into my own hands. Not that I wanted to deprive Cormac his fun, but I was wiped.

I stepped forward, and placed myself in front of Cormac, which he didn't care for one iota but I gave him my bitchiest I'm in charge right now stare before I turned back to the top dog in charge.

"Listen buddy, I've had a really long day and you are standing in between me and my beauty sleep. All this doesn't just happen on its own." Normally that statement would've made sense since I was an attractive girl, but standing there as I looked now just recently back from the edge of death, I couldn't quite pull it off. "I usually look much better, but whatever, you can either agree to set something up later where you can discuss your concerns or I can make you kneel at my feet in agony."

He decided to take a step in my direction. I had a feeling he was having an issue with backing down from a woman, especially in front of all the other wolves looking on.

I was getting ready to go all super Alchemist ninja when a pair of hands around my waist moved me to the side.

"Cormac, I'm telling you, I've got this!" I said as he moved in front of me.

He ignored me as he took the lead wolf in his grip and dangled him a foot off the ground. I heard an inhuman growl and I didn't think it was coming from the wolf in his hands.

There were still a healthy amount of them left. If he was going to pick through them one at a time, this could take a while.

Knowing we hadn't opened a wormhole in a while, I figured it was safe to play around. I just prayed a bystander didn't pop his head in as I concentrated my energy on starting one not even five feet from us.

"Excuse me," I said, to get the few heads that hadn't turned after it opened, to look. Play nice or that's your new home."

Cormac dropped the wolf, who fell to his knees before he stood. I probably should have kept my eyes on the wormhole. I might have known why the guys all ran then, but hey, I was the queen of opening up portals. I didn't need to look.

When their faces all dropped, I thought they were in awe of my wormhole skills. It wasn't until Cormac yelled to shut it that I realized something else was amiss. The biggest, ugliest creature I'd ever seen was walking through the wormhole I'd just created. It was at least ten feet tall and had leathery skin that glistened. No eyes but various marble looking black orbs all over its head spaced a couple of inches apart.

"Shut it," Cormac said again, and nudged me

jolting me from my shock.

I felt a twinge of guilt as I shut the portal, knowing I'd probably just killed whatever that was, but who could take the chance? Even with no visible mouth to be seen, I swear it had been sneering at us.

I scanned the alley a few times to reassure myself it was indeed gone. "What the hell was that?"

"No clue, but the wolves are gone," Cormac said as we stood in the alley.

"You know, I had them on the ropes, even without the monster."

"I swear you are going to be the death of me."

CHAPTER ELEVEN

"Are you going to tell me how you managed to survive last night?" Cormac asked as he handed me a latte as I sat up in bed. Thank God he didn't sit on the bed with me. I was still trying to process the kiss. Currently, we were both acting like it hadn't happened.

"I told you what happened. I don't know how I did it any more than you do. Wish I did."

Cormac leaned his shoulder against the wall, an intense look in his icy blue eyes.

"Where's Lacey?" I asked, not ready to talk about the elephant in the room.

"Lacey is safely away from here with her family."

"Where?"

"Are you sure you want to know? I wish I didn't, but Dodd told me before I could stop him."

I thought about it for a minute and said no. If the senator had some sort of ability of mind control, like it seemed he did, it wasn't safe. Just because he hadn't controlled mine yet didn't mean he couldn't. The less people that knew, the better. I was relieved and saddened at the same time that Lacey was gone.

"Does she and her family have enough to start over?"

"More than enough." He took a sip of his own latte, the look still there but I guess he wasn't looking to rush into a conversation about us either. "The wolves called. They want a sit down."

"And?"

"I told them we'd meet them in an hour, neutral location."

"We?"

"We are partners, aren't we?" A small smile flashed across his face before he left.

I stepped into the penthouse living room twenty minutes later, ready to go in what I considered my best business casual outfit of straight cut black slacks and a silky button down shirt. I wasn't sure if I should go for bad ass or corporate, but since the alley scene last night I figured maybe I should play up the brains aspect. This was my 'yes, I can kick your ass, but don't take it personally, it's just business' outfit.

"Cormac said he'd be right back and that you should eat this before you go."

"Hi Dark." I hadn't even noticed him at the table in the corner where a makeshift desk had been set up for him. His head was bent over, his concentration alternating between the book and the lap top. "How's it going? Anything?"

"Yes, the dialect sucks. The guy that wrote this had to be more boring than watching grass grow and he was convinced that The Keepers were going to bring about our version of the apocalypse."

"How far through the book are you?"

"Only about a quarter."

"You find anything else out about the monster yet?" Cormac asked as he walked in to the room and I took a quiet bite of the turkey club that had been waiting for me.

"No. They have no idea how it was made, just that it was supposed to cure all human kind, werewolf and Fae of disease."

"Do they explain how?" I asked.

"Nope, that might have actually been interesting, They just write that The Keepers are touting this to all the other races. Then something goes wrong."

"What?" I asked.

"They don't know."

"Keep reading," Cormac told Dark and then turned to me. "We've got to go,"

"So where's this neutral location we are heading to?"

"It's a diner, out on the highway, a few miles before the California border."

"And it's safe?"

"I'm not worried about a few wolves. As long as there are no snipers, we're good and I've already had the area swept."

"Why are snipers so bad?"

"Too many bullets, too swiftly, before we know they're coming; they take us down quicker than anything else. Always sweep an area for snipers. Always."

We walked into the garage where all his cars were stored and I looked at the space my trailer had occupied. Didn't matter, I'd find it.

"The Ferrari again?" I asked as he climbed into the silver sports car.

He opened up the engine and let it roar in the garage. Then smiled at me. "If I can afford it, and I love it, why shouldn't I? There are certain perks to being able to create gold. Why not enjoy them?"

I swear he drove quicker than normal as we headed out onto the open highway, just to show off, because I'd made a point of picking on his car.

"As to the many perks of being an Alchemist, I'm really not going to age?"

"No. For the same reason your breasts are a full C cup. Your brain decided what it thought was best and did it. Most male alchemists don't look older than thirty, the women seem to get stuck somewhere in between mid to late twenties."

"I'm not a full C."

"Just because you try to squeeze them into B's doesn't make it true."

"How do you know?"

"I know. Do you really want the details?"

I dropped the matter.

We pulled into the mostly empty parking lot. I felt a shudder in the ground as we stepped out of the car. "Was that an earthquake?"

"Felt like a small one."

"Weird timing." We'd had earthquakes before so it wasn't a big deal other than the fact that it was right before this meeting. "Who's here?"

"Rogo. That's the name of the guy you made pee his pants last night with the alien in the portal."

"I guess we're off to a good start."

He walked in first, paused just inside the door and checked out the place. It was the little things, like that, that were slowly wearing down my resolve against him. I didn't need him to protect me, but it didn't make a difference. The girly side of me went to pure mush and then my mind wandered back to the kiss. What the hell were we anymore? Friends…kinda? I guess? Partners? It seemed that way. Dating? No, definitely not. But what was the kiss then? All I knew was that I wasn't going to ask. The guy had shot me, then flirted with my best friend, then stole my trailer and he funniest thing was that I couldn't decide which of those was the worse deed.

When I stepped into the diner, Rogo was sitting in the corner booth with an attractive woman. How cute. It could be an interplanetary double date.

Up close, the woman was striking. Black straight hair fell to her waist as they both stood and shook our hands. Her name was Carlene and Rogo slung an arm possessively around the back of her seat when they sat down. I thought I'd picked up a bit of a sexist vibe from some of the wolves but the fact that he brought a female with him to this meeting made me soften slightly. Or maybe 'not quite as repulsed' might have been a more fitting description.

After the waitress brought us coffee and walked away, Rogo leaned forward. It wasn't exactly aggressive, but he was definitely trying to display dominance. Rogo could have beaten his chest like an ape and it wouldn't have made a difference. I guess that's the difference between people that are born to it or not.

"The wolves have elected me to be in charge, since Tracker is no longer available to speak for us." A pointed look toward me made it more than clear who he thought was responsible for that absence. "We have two issues."

"I'm listening." Cormac leaned back in a completely relaxed position. And was that his arm, slung on the back of my seat?

"You stole from us."

"I wouldn't describe it as *stealing*. It wasn't your history," I said. Cormac, on the other hand, said nothing. I knew it was a flimsy argument but I didn't have much to go on. Cormac's jaw was locked into place. If I thought he didn't like the Fae, they were best buddies compared to his reaction to Rogo. I found his demeanor grating as well.

Rogo sat there for a moment and fiddled with his silverware. I guessed he was debating whether or not he was going to take the straw I handed him and try to retain some pride, or if he was going to go to the mat with Cormac. Considering how I'd shamed him last night, it was a bitter pill. Finally, he nodded and looked like he was going to move on from it.

"The bigger issue we have is the portal being shut down."

Hmmm, nice touch. Downplay your failure with the book like it was the lesser issue. He might have made a decent politician. Maybe, when we killed the senator, we could nominate him for senate. It might be an improvement from the current political environment.

"Non-negotiable at present," Cormac replied and I hoped he was going to continue on and throw him a bone. Another full out slight would force Rogo's hand and then I'd either be opening up a portal that would eat up the diner or I'd be picking pieces of Rogo off the floor.

Just when I thought it was going to get ugly, Cormac handed him a salve for his pride. "But we can offer you extended visas while we are shut down."

Huh? Of course they can stay. We can't send them back! I wondered if there was even a reason we came today.

"That's reasonable," Rogo answered.

The coffee I'd just taken a sip of almost went spewing across the table. I swallowed it, but barely as half when down the wrong pipe. I went into a mindless coughing fit and excused myself from the table as Cormac and Rogo talked over some mindless and inconsequential details. I pointed toward the door and waited outside.

I watched as Cormac strode out of the diner. He didn't look as pleased as I thought he should've, since the meeting had gone better than anyone could've expected. I hopped off the hood and got back in the car. "What was the point of that whole thing, because I'm not getting this?" I said once we were back in the car.

"Remember all those new faces at Burrom's?"

"Of course."

"He's getting them in."

Shit. How the hell had I missed that? "He *wanted* you to think you'd won. You wanted him to think you won as well."

"Exactly. This meeting was a farce on every angle. If he had put up a fight I would've known he had nothing to do with it, but he rolled over."

"You think Hammond is alive and still out there, helping them?"

"He's alive. He must be. I just don't think that the defectors that left would have had the juice to do it."

"And we haven't been shut down long enough for it have gotten easier for them, yet."

"We've got to shut Hammond down. Without him, they're dead in the water."

Words failed me as the truth of it sank in. I didn't know why it bothered me. I'd helped almost kill Hammond, Father or not; had I expected him to run and find me afterward? We were on different sides in a war, and yet it still stung. It didn't make sense. I guess things didn't always need to make sense to hurt.

"Jo?"

"I'm fine." I wasn't. I felt another crack in the mortar chip off my wall. That's another thing about cement walls, once they start to crack, it always spreads. Problem with them is, it's not like you can go back to before you had the wall. No, now you just have a big messed up landscape with clumps of cement all over the place. "Next time, you better fill me in."

"Because you clue me into your plans?"

I didn't fight with him because I knew the only place it would end was some agreement on both our parts to full disclosure. I wasn't sure I was ready for that. I'd rather be in the dark every now and then.

We slowed to a stop as a line of cars spread out in front of us, with no end in sight.

"What's going on?" I asked, trying to peer over the truck in front of us, which was very hard to do in a Ferrari and when you're barely off the ground.

"I don't know. Can you drive a stick?"

"Not very well."

"Hop in the driver seat and move the car up if we start moving." He was opening the car door and was getting ready to step out.

"I said I CAN'T drive a stick," but he'd already gotten out as I said it. "And people wonder why I repeat myself. Obviously, I have to."

I grabbed the keys from the ignition, just in case someone else here could drive a stick and decided to take the opportunity, and I followed him. As soon as I got to the side of the road, I could see how far the line of cars went. I could barely make out where the line stopped.

Cormac turned and stopped when he heard me, waiting for me to catch up. There was a look in his eyes that chilled me, probably because I felt it too. There was something very wrong here. Not like a car accident wrong, I could feel it in the air. It even smelled weird.

The sun beat down on us as we walked further

up. We weren't the only ones walking. The closer we got, the more people I saw, all headed in the same direction, to find out what was going on. Now that I thought of it, I hadn't seen any traffic coming from the opposite direction in some time and then it struck me that I hadn't heard any sirens. Why weren't there any police or fire on their way to whatever calamity had occurred to stop a major roadway like this?

On a hunch, I pulled out my phone. "There's no cell service."

"Sometimes it's sketchy over here."

"You know that's not what it is," I told him.

First, I saw the people; there had to be at least a hundred of them all gathered. I realized most of the cars were abandoned by this point, their owners all searching for the problem like we were. I was worried, but not as alarmed as I was when I realized the air and sky past them didn't seem right. The closer we got, the more it appeared to take on a grayish murky appearance. With each step, it grew darker, until we were standing on the edge of an abyss like I'd never seen before. It was as large as five football fields and dome shaped. One gigantic wormhole stood open, in the middle of the desert, looking out onto pure space, interstellar space clouds and all. I tried to feel with my Keeper senses for the edges of this wormhole, but it didn't have a normal perimeter. It wasn't an area being forced and held open like we did when we traversed them, it was a violent rip. There was no closing this wound. Nothing to close it with. It was the difference between a razor slicing your skin and a wild beast tearing away a chunk of flesh, muscle and all, from your body.

Our universe had been mauled.

I looked for an opening in the crowd, where I could get a better look, but Cormac's hand on my arm stopped me.

"I don't think it's a good idea to get too close."

I stopped because I knew he was right, even though my curiosity compelled me to step closer. This thing was pumping out radiation that would be lethal to even a Keeper if we lingered. I looked at the people gaping at the monstrosity in all it's beautiful glory and knew they were dead men walking, every one of them. They simply didn't know yet.

"All these people…" I didn't finish my sentence.

"There's nothing to be done."

I looked away from them and focused on his face. I wanted to look anywhere but at them. I saw the regret I felt in his eyes.

I angled my head back in the direction we had come from. We needed to get out of there and figure out what happened. He paused, taking in the scene one last time and then walked with me.

"Other openings are doing this," I said, once we were a few hundred feet away.

Cormac didn't reply. He didn't need to. I knew he didn't know the exact reasoning behind the way portals had to be operated, only that they had certain parameters that needed to be upheld or there could be dire consequences. These parameters had been passed down, verbally, through generations. We had known there could be explosions, but I didn't even think Cormac had been aware of this possibility. It was hard to tell because he was back in stone faced mode. I was starting to wonder if that was, in part, for me. He had to be freaked out. There was a gas nebula sitting in the middle of Nevada. It was impossible to *not* be freaked out.

I pulled my phone back out but still, nothing. In the larger scheme of things, it was my smallest problem, but man did I hate being phoneless. With everything else going on, I needed my bars to show up or I might completely snap. I held it up in every funny direction possible as we walked back.

"Jo?"

"Yeah?" I answered, distracted and clinging to my phone and what felt like the last shred of my sanity.

"Don't lose it."

I stopped, looked at him and took a deep breath. He didn't have to say anything else. Things were getting uglier by the second. The people that could, or would, help were few in numbers. I was one of those very few and among the stronger of them, at least in certain areas. I couldn't lose it. If I did, the hole would become that much deeper and there were a hell of a lot of innocent people that had no clue what was happening. People that were closer and closer to a world of utter mayhem if we couldn't stop this train from derailing. I nodded and slipped my phone into my back pocket.

It was time to step up. If I couldn't handle it, who would?

CHAPTER TWELVE

The Ferrari completely sucked at off-roading and we had to abandon the car. Cell service came back after we'd gotten about five miles away from the space hole. 'Space hole' wasn't the most creative name for it, but it was better than *goddamn mother fucking thing that popped a hole in my world*. Even shortening that into an acronym would still have been a tongue twister, so space hole would have to do.

Like I was saying, five miles out and we'd been able to get Dodd on the phone. He'd personally flown a helicopter out to get us. Cormac had taken the controls and flown us back. Nobody had bothered to tell me The Lacard had a helicopter pad on top of the garage parking lot. You'd think someone might have mentioned it when I'd complained about UFOs waking me up in the middle of the night when my trailer had been there.

Considering what I knew about aliens, I'd found it rude of them to have laughed at the idea.

"Should we order up some food?" I asked, looking at the barren conference room I'd never seen before, located two floors below Cormac's penthouse.

"Yes, I'm starving!" Dodd was always starving and always stealing the food off my plate.

"How many do we have coming?"

"Vitor, his mother and cousin. Burrom and his second. Rogo..." Cormac started to rattle off.

"Why is he coming? You didn't tell me you were asking him."

"Because whether he admits it or not, he helped make that mess out in the desert. He can deny it all he wants, but he better pitch in and figure out how to clean the shit up."

"Okay, I can live with that. Who else?"

"Rogo and his seconds. I asked Sabrina to come up."

As soon as he said Sabrina, my eyes shot to Dodd. He wouldn't admit it but I knew he had a thing for her. It was a bit shocking, considering how respectable she was. I wondered if he knew he'd probably have to take her to dinner.

"Oh yeah, I asked Dark to come as well," Cormac said. Dark was growing on everyone, including me. "I think it might help him decipher the events in the book if he knows what's going on."

"I'm confused about one thing. Who's in charge of the Fae? Is it Vitor of Burrom?"

"Technically, Vitor. But if you want something Fae related done, you go to Burrom."

"Then why would we go to Vitor to break the initial contract for the portal?"

"Because his ancestors forged the contract. The magic would respond better to him. He'd be able to sense the connection easier, as well."

"And what about Keepers? Did your ancestors help forge the original contract?"

"No, but yours did. Hammond is the second generation of Drake. I'm still wondering if that had something to do with the events of the evening."

I knew he was referring to the magic tethers.

"Are Burrom and Vitor cool with each other?"

"On the surface, yes. Deep down?" Dodd made a stabbing motion accompanied by the Pyscho sound when Norman Bates stabs his mother.

"Gotcha. Where're Buzz and Ben?"

"I sent them out to the other portal locations. I want to make sure they are completely shut down."

Sabrina showed up just as the food came, looking stunning in a red suit, her thick chestnut hair brushing her shoulders. Dodd definitely noticed how good she looked too.

Vitor and his family arrived at the same time as Burrom and his entourage. I thought that Burrom was only bringing one other, but maybe he wanted more numbers. I'd never seen Vitor and Burrom together. There was a tense moment as I wondered if they were going to fight over the seat at the foot of the table. I found it telling how no one tried to take the head chair.

I think they were leaving it in respect for Cormac, but he didn't sit down. I took the head chair instead. Why shouldn't I? The freak senator was more my problem than anyone else's.

Everyone settled in and I felt a shift on my chair as Cormac leaned his forearms on the top of it. All eyes were on him, then me, then him again. No. It probably didn't look as bad as I thought. I was just being overly sensitive. He probably didn't even realize how it looked.

"I'm sure everyone in this room knows why I called this meeting," he opened. All eyes moved to Rogo, his girlfriend Carlene, and the other guy he'd brought, who'd been introduced as Mace.

"We didn't do anything!" Rogo stood when he said it and at that moment, I thought all chances of having a peaceful meeting were through.

The Fae, strangely in unison now, stood as well and I thought some ugly shit was about to break out. I still hadn't seen them in action. A hazy aura started to grow around Burrom and I was almost hoping he would show a few of his talents. I didn't care for Rogo anyway and I was dying with curiosity. Dodd jumped to his feet. It might have been to get ready to break up a brawl or hop in for some fun.

Every Fae in the room started yelling back at Rogo, and his crew, that they were to blame. They screamed back that the Fae were elitists and had no idea what they spoke of. They continued back and forth with who was doing what, until I couldn't make out what anyone was screaming anymore. I slumped in my chair, ready to let them all fight it out. It was clear the anger in this room went much deeper than the space hole eating up Nevada.

"Stop." It wasn't a scream, but somehow everyone heard it and turned toward Cormac. "It doesn't matter who's to blame for this thing. Right now, we need to get it under control so that we don't have any more. We can place blame later."

"How do we know she didn't make it?" Rogo said, looking at me. "We know how she makes wormholes anywhere she wants to."

"Hey, dumb dumb! Why would I trash my own planet?"

I heard Cormac clear his throat from behind me, indicating he wasn't thrilled with my approach when he was trying to form some sort of unity.

"It's not my fault if he's going to say stupid things," I directed back at Cormac.

"How do we know it's your planet? I heard about some other things you've done that aren't exactly human, are they? I don't even think she should be here. She might be behind all of this. No one knows her. She shows up out of nowhere and we are supposed to trust her?"

All eyes were on me now. I looked around the room and Burrom wasn't looking at me. Rogo stared accusingly along with his people.

"You are doing some very unpredictable things," Vitor said in an apologetic voice.

Even Dodd raised his eyebrows when I looked at him. "Oh no, don't take that the wrong way," he said when I gaped at him. "I've got your back one hundred percent. But you've got to admit, they make a pretty good case."

"That does not make me feel better!"

"I thought we were being honest?"

"It doesn't matter what anyone thinks," Cormac said, "she's with me and that means she stays."

With me? I don't blush. Haven't in years but I swear he would be the downfall of my twenty year run. He's got to be doing this on purpose.

Then I felt his hand on my shoulder. Okay, he was just stressing his solidarity with me, not marking his claim. When I heard Dodd snicker to my right I wanted to belt him, but it would just make the situation more awkward than it already was. I had to settle for kicking him under the table.

He gave me a look that said *that was mean*. Then I rolled my eyes towards the doctor and smirked.

He stopped laughing.

"Portals are being opened. I don't care how or why, right now. I just need to know where and I need them shut down immediately, before we end up with another hole somewhere."

The room fell quiet and everybody again eyed up Rogo and his people.

"It wasn't me," he said defensively. I still didn't like him, but I believed him.

I stood up and walked closer to his chair and swung it around to face me, daring either anyone to try to stop me. I hovered over him."You know who and where, though, don't you."

His girlfriend growled but remained seated. His other comrade, Mace, didn't even bother to growl. Rogo looked scared. They knew they were outnumbered and no one, not Cormac or the Fae, would interfere if I let loose a little pain on them.

"It was already going on when I took leadership. I had no part in starting it up."

"Who did?" Cormac asked, from over my

shoulder. I hadn't even seen him move in.

"That politician guy. He had it running way before I got voted in."

"Why? What did he want in return?"

"He said he wanted nothing."

"And you believed him?" The sarcasm dripped off my tongue like a sweet claret wine.

"No," he shot back. "I just couldn't stop it."

"I thought you were their leader now?" I said. "Doesn't that mean you call the shots?"

"It doesn't work like that with the wolves," Dark started to explain.

I stepped back and looked at Dark, more interested in what he had to say than Rogo.

"You don't speak for us anymore." The venom in Rogo's tone was lethal and he stood now to lean over the table in a threatening manner toward Dark.

"He speaks for me," Cormac interjected as he grabbed Rogo's shirt and shoved him back into his seat.

Rogo looked pissed but he didn't say a word. I guess Dark was officially with us.

"Is he doing it alone?" Cormac pressed Rogo.

"No, he's got one of your guys. Hammer something or other."

"Hammond," I corrected. Every Fae in the room looked at me, but no one said a word. I went from being an orphan to having a father who was teamed up with a monster and destroying Earth. It just kept getting better and better. "Do you know where he is?"

"No, but I can find him pretty easily."

"Do it." I anticipated a fight, but he simply

nodded and I went back to my chair, not wanting to be that close to him anymore, Cormac following me like some sort of bodyguard I neither needed or wanted.

Cormac stepped up to the table and leaned his hands on the surface. "On to the next problem. Does anyone know what the senator actually is? He's got human records but we all know how easy it is to build a fake past." His eyes shot to me. "He's anything but human."

"You mean besides that your people made him?" Vitor asked.

"Yes, something helpful would be good. Especially since you seem to like our planet so much, I'm sure you don't want your new home trashed either."

I looked around the room. "How does no one have any idea? Rogo, your people were working with him. You had the closest contact. You know nothing?"

"He only came around once or twice. Haven't seen him since and I already asked around. And as Vitor just said, you guys made him and don't know. How the hell should we?"

"See? He does make a pretty good case sometimes, even for being an idiot," Dodd said softly to me.

"Whatever. He's still a dick," I whispered back.

"A dick with really good hearing," Rogo said from across the length of the table.

I didn't apologize. He was a dick.

Cormac cleared his throat and I swear it was to disguise his own laughter. "We need to take him down."

"What about the hole?" Burrom asked.

"We make sure all portals are shut down and we hope we don't get anymore."

"Can she fix it?" he asked and pointed to me.

"No, I can't. Not alone, anyway. It isn't a normal wormhole where you can just press it open and once you release the pressure, it closes. This is a tear."

"Another reason that we need to work together to take him down." Cormac stood up again and walked toward Sabrina. "What about the radiation it's releasing?"

"It's fine for everyone in this room as long as we don't linger near it too long."

"And what about regular humans?"

"Not so much. You'd have to cordon off a twenty mile area in every direction. Even further, eventually, if it keeps radiating at this rate."

"They've got NASA all over the place. I'll make some calls to my connections to make sure it happens, if they haven't already figured that out."

We knew the place had been swarmed by government within the first few hours. Unlike the mountain collapse, they didn't even try to put out a phony press release for this. They pretended it wasn't happening. I didn't blame them. It was hard to talk your way out of a gaping space hole and not have people think the world was ending.

"Rogo, anyone that has ever had any interaction with the senator - I want sent over here for questioning. Vitor, Burrom, talk to all your elders that are on this side. I need any information they can give us."

The fighting was over as they all realized the dire situation and slowly let out of the room. I think most were feeling as deflated as I was, no closer to a solution than when we started. I leaned back and crossed my ankles on the conference table, not ready to move, as my brain sought a solution that I knew I didn't have.

Alone in the room with only Cormac now, while Dodd walked them out with Sabrina, I wanted at least some answers from someone. "Why did you make it look like we were together?"

He looked at me as if I was crazy and smiled. "I didn't."

"Yes, you did."

"No, I didn't. I think you're reading into things."

"You are really saying you didn't?" I repeated, starting to feel a bit foolish and a tinge embarrassed. Could I have been letting my own feeling taint the way I saw his actions?

"That's exactly what I'm saying." He walked over and sat on the table near my ankles. Lifting them up he towed my chair closer to him until he was close enough to lean down over me and put a hand on each chair arm. "Did you want me to stake my claim on you?"

"That isn't what I said."

"I think it's what you want though."

"No, it isn't."

He was still smiling as if he didn't believe it, but there was something else in his eyes that I found unsettling. "This isn't the time for playing around,

Cormac."

"There's always time to play."

His phone vibrating on the table next to him saved me from making a complete fool of myself as I melted into a puddle of lust.

"What's wrong?" I asked, as I saw him read a message.

"I don't know yet." He dialed in a number and I was a bit surprised when he did so on speaker. "Buzz, what's up?"

"Another one just happened."

"You mean what I think?" Cormac asked, clearly not wanting to put it into words on the phone.

"Yes. And it's twice the size."

"Where?"

"About seventy miles north east of our location."

"But that would put it…"

"Yes. It's bad…real bad."

"We're on our way." I looked at his face as he pushed end on his phone.

"Where we going?"

"New York City. Or what's left of it."

CHAPTER THIRTEEN

News had spread like crazy within minutes. Twitter and all the social media were alight with the fact that NYC was now completely gone. A private jet flew us to a landing strip in New Jersey, where Buzz and Ben waited for us. It was seven hours later and the small, private airport was somewhere in between a state of great urgency and disorganized mayhem. People of means waited on the tarmac in their private planes, trying to get the hell out of Dodge. According to the ground crew, there wasn't a commercial flight to be had. Their phones were ringing off the hook with people trying to get a charter but there wasn't a plane left. Cormac had the crew lock ours down in a maintenance garage, out of sight, to make sure it would be there when we got back.

We took a yacht from a small seaside town in NJ called Middletown. It was even crazier there. People walking quickly down the docks, loading up their belongings onto their boats. I'd never seen anything like it in my life. Watching them hurry their children aboard, heading off to anywhere but there, a place so close to what was once NYC.

I wanted to stop them and tell them everything would be okay.

I couldn't. It might not be.

It didn't take very long to sail close enough to see that NYC was truly gone. Gone. Just gone.

From what Buzz had said, it had happened in a matter of seconds. He'd been close enough at the time to see it. It was there, and then it wasn't. Millions of people were just gone. Skyscrapers disappeared into nowhere. The entire city, and parts of the New Jersey coastline, across the river, were now torn from our universe, leaving a gaping hole where stars from another place and time hung. It looked too beautiful for something that was so deadly.

We bobbed in the ocean for a while, the four of us just staring. I don't know why exactly we couldn't stop looking but we stayed there and stared for a while before we could speak. Shock, disbelief, grief, and maybe most of all…dread of what was to come; all those things ran through my brain.

"What does this one feel like to you?" Cormac finally broke the silence to ask.

"I don't know," I replied and wiped away a tear that had finally managed to escape. I'd thought I'd done away with those completely. I guess if it was bad enough, there were still more to be had. "How does it feel to you?"

"Your senses are much better than mine when it

comes to wormholes, but to me it feels ragged and irregular, more so than the last one."

I reached out my senses to it, like someone would take a deep breath trying to catch a scent on the air. "Yes. Ragged edges. Even stronger radiation."

"Do you think you could close it?"

I shook my head, annoyed he'd even asked. I hadn't been able to close the one in Nevada. Didn't he think I would have done, if I could? There wouldn't have been a discussion about when or how. I would've just done it. When I felt this one and applied any sort of pressure, it didn't budge.

"What about if we had more Keepers trying at once?" he suggested.

"I have no idea." I closed my eyes, not wanting to look anymore. "I'm sorry, I just have no idea."

"Trust me, I get it."

"The edges feel torn, not distorted. If we try to force it closed, I'm not sure what will happen. I couldn't do it by myself, anyway. I'd need help. We'd have to force it closed and the way it feels, I just don't know if it's going to be possible. We'd be stretching the very matter of our universe."

"This is worse than the last. If we don't close it, I'm not sure what will happen." His words didn't give details but his tone spelled it out clearly.

"You mean…like everything?"

"We gotta try," Buzz said, as if he had just woken up.

Ben was still transfixed. There was no judgment from me. This was my second space hole and I didn't think I'd be any less stunned or horrified if it had been my hundredth.

"How many Keepers are there?" I'd only met fifteen, but I didn't know how many there were at the other locations.

"Not every Keeper can work a wormhole. There are forty-seven, excluding you and I, that can do it with varying degrees of strength and ability. There are about twenty-four more that can't but have other skills."

"I don't think it's going to be enough. We need more. What about the people you lost to Tracker and Hammond?"

He didn't answer.

"Cormac?"

"Twenty-two."

"We need them. It's no worse than working with Rogo."

"Yes, it is. Rogo was never with me."

"If we can get them, we've got to use them."

"Fine, but keep them away from me." He turned as he said, "We've got to get going. I'm afraid that if we don't get back soon, there won't be a plane to get back to." Cormac walked back and started up the boat engine.

I sat and watched the spot where NYC used to be fade into the distance as everyone fell silent again. It broke my heart. Watching a civilization falling apart will do that to you.

It was a good thing the airport wasn't far from the dock because the traffic had reached a notch below gridlock. The radio had nothing but people screaming the sky was falling. Even satellite radio had interrupted service to talk about the catastrophe.

Some said it was aliens, some said it was the government, or the Chinese government, or Russians. The list went on and on trying to find a logical place to lay blame.

The president came on and told everyone to remain calm. That they were getting the situation under control. It was laughable. How did you get missing parts of your universe under control? Once we got close enough to the airport, we abandoned the car and walked the rest of the way. I was relieved to not have to listen to the radio anymore.

It took six hours to get back from NJ in the small private jet. The first couple of hours I'd been despondent. By hour three, the ugly reality of what was happening to our world clung to me like the death stench of the black plague finding its latest victim. By time we landed, I was beyond all reason. I was pure fury.

When the door of the penthouse clicked shut behind Buzz, it was just Cormac and I left in the room. I'd found my bulls eye. If he hadn't been running portals, none of this would've happened. I'd be in med school, blissfully ignorant, and millions of people would still be alive. Earth wouldn't be on the verge of destruction.

I started pacing as he flipped through paperwork on the table. Even that bugged me. Who gave a shit about paperwork? My world is about to fall apart and he's flipping through papers? "You know this is your fault? You and your goddamn wormholes. You had no right to bring aliens here. The senator wouldn't even have existed if it weren't for your people."

He dropped the papers onto the table and went still. "And you have no blame here?"

"I didn't start this! I don't run this."

"I took over from my ancestors…as did you."

"Don't compare us."

"Can't I? What have you been doing for the last several weeks? If you found it so appalling, why did you join us?"

"I never joined you."

"The facts would say otherwise."

"This is your fault!" I screamed.

"Come here," he said and crooked his finger.

"Why?" I asked, suddenly thrown off guard.

"Come here."

"No. What do you want?" I took a few steps backward as he inched forward. "What?" I asked again, panic surging through me.

Then he lunged at me, taking me with him to the floor as he took the hit for us both.

"What are you doing?" I asked again as he kept his arms circled around me.

"I'm giving you what you asked for."

"I didn't ask to be tackled to the ground and hugged," I told him as I started to squirm about.

"Yes, in Jo language, this is exactly what you were asking for. If you keep squirming, you might get everything you've been asking for."

He rolled me underneath him and his hips ground against mine as my breath caught in my throat. His mouth covered mine, his tongue dipping erotically into my mouth.

"I never asked for this." The words didn't sound very convincing, said on a breathy sigh when he pulled back slightly.

"If it's not what you wanted, then why aren't you telling me to stop?"

"Because you're a lot bigger than I am."

His hand came up and grazed my face. "If you wanted me off of you, all you'd have to do is ask."

His face hovered mere inches above mine, his pale blue eyes staring into my green. I turned my face to the side. I didn't want him to leave me. He was right. Whatever this was...I wanted it. Not just sex, I craved the comfort I felt from his closeness. But after everything that had gone between us, how could I even think of letting it happen?

I kept my face turned; I couldn't accept him and yet I couldn't push him away. I was in emotional purgatory. He leaned his face down, grazing my ear slightly with his lips. I closed my eyes, enjoying the sensation but knowing I should stop it.

"I don't think..."

"Jo," his voice interrupted me. "I'm sorry. I'd give anything to undo it." The stubble of his jaw grazed along my neck as he rested his forehead in my hair.

A knot formed in my throat as I listened to him. I knew what he was talking about but I needed to confirm it anyway. "You're sorry you had people shot?" I asked, hiding behind a group because I couldn't confront it head on.

"No, only you." His lips pressed against my neck as he whispered again, "I only regret you."

"Why?" It was a simple question and the one I wanted answered most.

I felt his head shake back and forth. "I just

didn't know."

Of all the things he could've said, those words skewered me.

I felt his head lift and I thought he was going to rise, but instead I felt his lips at the base of my throat. First his lips and then his teeth were grazing over my skin, inch by slow inch until he reached the corner of my jaw. I heard myself moan as he settled further in between my legs.

Push him off, I kept telling myself, but I didn't. I turned my head instead and met his lips. I realized quickly that he'd been waiting for something from me as his lips sought mine with a deep hunger, stealing the breath from my lungs. His hips ground into mine and I threw my head back on a moan as his hand sought my breast and his breath seared my throat.

I heard a person clear their throat that wasn't Cormac. Like I didn't have enough issues with intimacy, I needed to get caught laying on the floor by…I didn't even know. I turned my head to see Cormac already staring at Vitor, Buzz and a strange little woman who looked oddly familiar.

"Sorry, but you said to bring anyone that had contact with the senator in right away." For an apology, Vitor didn't sound very apologetic.

"You could've knocked," Cormac said as he stood and offered me a hand up.

"Boss, normally you hear me get out of the elevator."

"From now on, knock." There was an edge to his voice that added *and drop it,* without saying it.

I pushed my hair out of my face as I looked at

the newcomers as if they hadn't just walked in on me laying flat on my back with Cormac between my legs. Try as I might, I couldn't stop thinking there was a certain reaction. Buzz had a slight twinkle in his eye, and Vitor looked...not so twinklish. The strange woman...she just looked odd. And where did I know her from? Then I remembered. When I had first started running the portal, she'd been one of my first travelers and had told me I looked familiar.

"This is Colie. She's of the Fae. She knew the senator."

"That I did," she said in a strange accent I hadn't heard from any of the Fae before. She stepped around the chair that still lay on the floor and made herself comfortable on the couch. "Strange thing, he was. Younger back then, but still an odd one."

"So he ages?" I asked.

"He's not human, if that's what you're trying to ask, but yes, he's aged."

"What is he?"

"That I don't know. But I do know a human when I see them. He ain't."

"How do you know him?"

Her eyes, with irises so dark they looked black, ran over my face. "My niece Malora brought him around a couple of times."

"Malora?" I repeated.

"Yes. I told you that you looked familiar," she said.

And that was it. No show of emotion about finding a long lost loved one. Nothing.

"You knew my mother?"

"Yes."

She didn't need to say anything more. I could tell the old woman had hated her.

"Are there any other relatives?"

"No. I'm it, and you should be grateful. Bad lot, the whole bunch of them. All dead now."

I wasn't sure how to react to her words, or the chill in her voice. I hadn't known my mother. Do you defend someone you never knew? What's the point? Everybody knows you don't have a leg to stand on and right now I needed information from her. I cared more about that than defending a stranger.

I sat down on the opposite couch to her; everyone else stood. As abrasive as this woman came across, I felt oddly sad for her. Even Vitor, her own kind, seemed to want to keep his distance and it wasn't from fear.

"Do you know what he was doing with Malora?" I had to concentrate to not trip over her name, feeling so odd speaking of her.

"No, but I'm sure it was no good. She had a tendency to hang around undesirables. Hanging with the wolves, and the lowest of them to boot. Always carrying on about all the secrets the wolves had. Like the Wolves knew things we didn't, hmmph. Then she started panting after a Keeper named Hammond. She could always get any man she wanted, with her looks. More of a curse than a gift, if you want my opinion."

Again, I felt her judgmental stare on me. Was I supposed to apologize for being attractive now? I was quickly losing any sympathy I had for the woman, ostracized or not. Plus, I was relieved Dark wasn't here right now to hear how she felt about the wolves. He'd become a staple in the penthouse.

"Malora was a tramp," she continued.

You need her information. You can tell her to get the hell out after you get her information, I repeated like a silent mantra in my head.

"She was trying to get knocked up by Hammond."

"Why do you say that?"

"Because when she couldn't get pregnant, she went to what you people would call a doctor to get spelled. That's when the senator guy came around. I only saw him a handful of times but she needed him for something. That's how Malora was. She didn't bother with anyone that didn't do something for her."

The idea I could somehow be the senator's daughter ran through my mind but then I remembered the blood. I was Hammond's, and for once, actually happy about it. That was bad enough. But what had Malora needed from the senator, I wondered; I asked the woman in front of me.

"I don't know. But she got something. He wouldn't have been around if she hadn't. My guess it had something to do with you. And Hammond."

"So what happened to him? Did he ever come around again?"

"I don't know. She disappeared right around the time I thought for sure she was pregnant. Never saw her again." The old woman looked around the room and waited. "No more questions?"

I shook my head. All the times I'd imagined talking to a family member and now I sat here and couldn't think of a single other question.

"We'll get in touch with you if we think of any," Cormac said.

Colie stood, paused by Vitor with her palm out and he placed a wad of cash into it. Burrom never would've of had to pay anyone. I'd seen him with his kind. There was a reverence and touch of fear.

Cash in hand, she walked out the door without a by your leave. Yes sir, that's my family.

"Now what?" It wasn't exactly a question but a statement, and no one answered me. "We still have no idea what he is. We have no clue how to kill him. I think the only option we've got is to out him."

"What is that going to do?" Vitor asked.

"I agree. We've got nothing else. Let's make it as hard as possible for him," Cormac said.

"I think he's afraid of being touched by me."

All three men turned to look at me.

"In the alley, when you got shot, it's just a hunch but I don't think he wanted me to touch him. I think he was actually afraid of me getting close to him. If we could corner him somewhere that he can't disappear, somewhere I can get my hands on him, maybe I could take him out."

"No, it's impossible," Cormac said at the same time Buzz and Vitor said "Yes."

"She's the only one that might be capable of closing wormholes of that size up. You want us to just walk her out there for the senator to kill her?"

"I'm doing it," I said as I dug into my position,

not sure if I was so adamant because I didn't like
Cormac trying to push his way or because of the
niggling fear that I was the last one in between the
senator and billions of humans.

Cormac stared me down as I stood. "I'm doing
it," I repeated, then in a softer voice I said, "we
don't have another option."

Dodd burst into the room, just as Cormac
opened his mouth to speak. "There's another one."

No one had to ask. We all knew what he was
talking about.

"It took out a chunk of Mexico. This one's got
about a ten mile radius," Dodd continued.

"How long ago?" I asked.

"Not more than five minutes. It's just hitting the
air waves now."

I walked over to the window overlooking the
strip and waited for the panic to descend. The
government had been able to keep the first, smaller
one a secret so far. The NY one had created pure
panic in the region but here, it hadn't been as bad.
People had thought it was a localized problem. Yes,
they'd been scared, but not the terror that would
soon grip them when they knew it wasn't local.
There would be nowhere safe.

As I watched below, I saw it begin. Humans
still have a pack mentality at their core. It pops up
in the strangest of places, if you look. On a summer
day, with no traffic, cars on the highway will still
drive in clusters, never really spaced apart evenly.
At the mall, shopping, people flock to where other
people are browsing, thinking it's where they should
be. In times of turmoil and stress, the instinct

increases tenfold. Our natural instincts come to the fore and drive our actions.

Slowly, the people on the street started to clump together. Strangers, who wouldn't normally approach each other, huddled together until there was barely a stray to be found. Soon, they'd start to hide indoors, probably in bomb shelters and basements, clinging to an imagined security like a child hides under their covers. I wished I was ignorant and thought I could hide from this. They were the lucky ones. We'd all meet our death, but I would watch its slow march forward.

CHAPTER FOURTEEN

"This is crazy," I said to no one in particular as we all walked down the Vegas Strip. It had only been yesterday that the latest space hole had appeared, and approximately twenty-four hours later the place was a ghost town. The casino was abandoned, with most of the staff having called out. The streets were deserted, shops were closed with handmade signs taped to the windows, declaring they were unsure of when they'd reopen.

The only ones that were outside were us. 'Us' felt like a school outing. The call came in from Rogo an hour ago, giving us Hammond's locale. It was strange how the timing of that call worked out. He just all of a sudden knew exactly where he'd be, as the Earth teetered on destruction because of what they had been doing.

I decided to ignore the coincidence for the moment and immediately went to leave. Cormac didn't want me to go alone. Even though he didn't want to see Hammond, he came. Buzz, Dodd, Ben and Dark decided to join in to see the downfall of society in person.

It felt like that too. Like society had decided to come to a screeching halt in the course of a single day.

"Do you think people are going to start looting?" Buzz asked.

"I think they're too scared to come out to loot," I replied. I hadn't even seen a police car, not that there was anyone to arrest.

"Where we walking?" Dodd asked.

"Caesar's," I replied.

"I can't believe that's the place he chose," Dodd continued. "I thought he hated that guy back when he knew him? What a hypocrite."

My head snapped quickly to Cormac. "Please tell me your birthday is at least A.D.?"

"Of course it is."

I heard Buzz humph from behind us and I swear he said something like 'yeah, not by much' under his breath. I turned back to look but they were all smiles. I've become a big fan of ignorance lately and I decided that moment was a good time to practice my new life plan of 'need to know only,' and sometimes not even then. If I had started this plan earlier in my life, right now I'd be watching Star Wars DVDs and eating cookie dough ice cream in a cozy little basement. My quest for knowledge had me tracking down the destroyer of the universe. You tell me who the bright ones are?

As we stood in front of Caesar's, I paused. This

was going to be awkward enough when I opened with "Hey Dad, how've you been since I buried you alive and left you for dead?" I wasn't looking for an audience.

"Guys?"

"No sweat," Dodd answered. "We'll hang back."

"Thanks."

I made my way into the casino with Cormac by my side. I'd known there was no way he'd wait, so I'd expected this, maybe even relied on it a bit, if I were feeling particularly truthful.

The lobby was empty but for two girls huddled behind the front desk listening to AM radio news. That creeped me out on a normal day, with its fuzzy transmission and newscasters who always sounded somber. They barely looked over as we walked in and I motioned them back to their radio. That was all they needed to ignore us again.

"I'm hoping you have an idea where the French Villa is in this place?"

"This way."

The place was deserted. I wondered why anybody had even opened the doors but I guess they still had a straggle of guests hidden away in their rooms with no way home. The car rentals agencies were depleted of vehicles and the airports had all shut down, the FAA grounding any non-emergency flights until further notice.

"I'll wait out here," Cormac said, once we stood outside the doors.

I pressed the bell and waited. After a few minutes, I pressed it again.

"Do you think he's in there and just not answering?"

"Come on."

"Where?"

"There's a balcony off the pool area. We'll go in that way."

The hottest day of the summer so far, and even the pool area was abandoned. Cormac waved me closer and I tried to not be self-conscious of the entire length of me touching him as we floated up to the balcony. I pulled back a little too quickly once our feet touched the landing; not because I wanted to, but because I didn't want him to know how much I liked being near him.

Cormac raised his nose to the air. "Do you smell that?"

I filled my lungs with air. "I can't smell anything. What is it?"

He tried the doors to the suite but predictably they were locked. I figured he'd just break the door down but instead he ran his hand over the joint where the door knob was and it melted.

"Can I do that? How did you do it?"

"I forced the particles in the metal apart, liquefying it. I don't know if you can do it but you've got a long time to try."

"Does that mean I'm going to need a long time?" I asked while he stuck his fingers in the hole where the door knob had been and opened it.

"I'm making no judgments." He took a step in the door and waited for me.

"That would be a first," I said as I followcd him into the opulent suite. "Wow, this place is nice."

"Overkill, if you ask me."

"This from the man with ten Ferraris."

"Different."

Cormac raised his nose into the air again and started walking toward a set of doors off the main living area.

"What is it?"

"Blood." He stalled at the doorway. "Maybe you should let me go first."

I didn't bother discussing it with him, just pushed forward.

"Shit." It wasn't the most eloquent reaction to finding Hammond dead, but I didn't know what else to say.

"Damn," Cormac said as he stepped into the room next to me.

Hammond was laid out on the bed, motionless, head on the pillow with a peaceful expression on his face. If it weren't for the foot long slices that ran up the insides of his forearms and the veins that were ripped out, hanging like strands of spaghetti, and the blood red circle of blood he lay on, it might not have been so bad.

"Are you okay?"

"It screws up the plans a bit. I was counting on his strength to help with the space hole tears."

"That isn't what I meant."

"I know." I walked closer, staring at the father I'd never get to know and wondered why he would do something like this. "Do you think it was definitely suicide?"

"I'd never have guessed that he'd go out this way, but yes. I think he did this himself." He paused over him.

"You think he left a note?" I asked Cormac who was already searching the room.

"Nothing here. I'll go check the rest of the place," he said, but then paused. "Why don't you help me look?"

"I want to take a couple of pictures on my phone."

"Of the body?"

"Yes. In case I'm missing something."

"I'll do that and you go check out the rest of the place."

"Cormac, what's the deal with you?"

"He was your father."

"No, he was a man that I never got to know, that most likely has the blood of millions on his hands." I looked down again at his body, hands lying in blood. "Bad choice of words, but you get my point."

"If you say you're good, okay." I thought he was going to just exit the room at that point but he still didn't leave, fussing here and there, opening more drawers.

"Cormac, I'm fine. Seriously," he nodded and finally moved on to the other rooms.

I watched his back retreat and pulled out my phone. I took a series of shots from every angle possible, even if some of the close ups made me feel ill. I didn't want to miss any clues if this turned out to not be a suicide.

"How's it coming along?" Cormac yelled from the other room. "I'm want to give the guys a call to get some help in here to take care of the evidence.

I'd prefer the hotel not find him."

"Go ahead," I yelled back. I continued taking pictures, trying to figure out what would've driven him to do something like this. Had he simply been blasé after all these years and lost the drive to keep going, or had there been something more devious at work? He'd had a certain zest about him when I'd met him. This just didn't sit right.

His body looked ashen already and I felt a sense of mourning creep upon me; I wanted to ignore it but couldn't completely squash the feeling. It wasn't for him; it was more a selfish mourning. He'd had a long and interesting life. Why couldn't I have shared in that, even for just a little while? These last weeks he'd been alive but hadn't reached out to me at all. It made me doubt that he hadn't known about me from the beginning. Maybe he had been mad about the mountain and he would've in time, but I'd never know now.

"Whoa," Dodd said as he walked in. "This is some serious shit. Now this…this is shit you don't come back from." He walked around the bed eyed up the scene. "You know, I'm surprised he didn't do it in the tub?"

"Why?"

"He was very neat. This just seems a bit… messy."

"Let's get him out of here," Cormac said as he walked back in. "Is Buzz getting a car?"

Dodd nodded as he started to roll Hammond up in the top blanket from the bed. Cormac and I both moved to the opposite side to start helping him when everything started to shake.

I grabbed the edge of the bed trying to keep from falling. "I don't think that's an earthquake." I gazed at Dodd and Cormac, praying they'd disagree.

Cormac looked at me. "It could have been, but I don't think it was."

Cormac answered his phone as it started to ring a second later. "Yes, here too. See what you can find out. We'll be there in a minute." He hung the phone up and threw it in his pocket. "Come on, let's get out of here. I don't want to be in this building when another one hits. Dodd, you get the body down, I'll take Jo."

Dodd swung Hammond up over his shoulder as he grumbled about how unfair life was sometimes.

We floated down to the abandoned pool and made our way through the back to where Dark and Buzz waited in a Mercedes truck. Hammond went into the trunk area and the three of us squeezed into the back seat.

I pulled my phone out, along with everyone but Buzz, and that was only because he was driving and Dark yelled at him about driving and surfing at the same time.

"I don't see anything about more holes, but according to what people are writing on Twitter, more than half of the globe felt the shaking," Dodd said.

"The holes are creating instabilities," I offered up.

"Then we've got to try to get them closed, like yesterday," Dark said.

I shook my head. "We've got to take out the senator first. If he's still helping someone open more behind the scenes, it will just keep getting worse anyway."

"So what do we do? The senator or try to fix the holes?" Buzz asked.

I looked over at Cormac who was suspiciously quiet, a pensive look on his face.

"Let's try to fix the smallest hole in Nevada with everyone we can get to help and see if it's even possible," I offered. "Then we plan to corner the senator. If we don't take him out soon and he opens up another one, we might not have anything left to fix."

CHAPTER FIFTEEN

Cormac had called contacts in NASA, the CIA and the FBI in order to get us close enough to the small space hole that ate up the Nevada desert. I'd heard him speak to dignitary after dignitary, pulling string after string, and all I'd really wanted to do was take the phone from his hands and scream loudly 'The gig's up boys and girls! Cut out the red tape, the ship is sinking!' I'd restrained myself, but barely.

Here we were, twenty Keepers dressed in black, slinking through the night like special ops on our way to save the Earth. I didn't know if there would be enough of us, but after the ground shook earlier today, I didn't want to wait for the rest of the Keepers to get here. Traveling was a real nightmare these days. No commercial planes, you had to travel with your own gas supply, if you were lucky enough to have one. Even with Cormac's private planes, we couldn't get them all here quick enough.

Better to try and come back if necessary. But I had to try. Waiting was no longer an option.

As we approached, the first thing that surprised me was that it was easier to see the thing at night. From a distance, it looked like a giant glowing orb, protruding right from the ground.

"You sure you're ready to try this?" Cormac asked as we neared its glowing brilliance.

"I didn't know there were other options."

We paused about five hundred feet from the rim. "I wish there was." Cormac's voice echoed the awe I felt inside. "I'm going to be on your right, Dodd and Buzz on your left."

"Why isn't Sabrina participating? She's a Keeper."

"I'd rather have her about one hundred feet behind us, waiting," he replied.

"Good idea. Once we get there, we've got to act quickly or I'm afraid the radiation will take us down before we can close anything."

We lined up in an arc, with me at dead center. Fitting place name, I thought. I hoped it wasn't foretelling.

"Okay everyone, once we hit ten feet, I'm going to channel all the energy through me and direct it towards the space hole. Let me lead, but everyone concentrate on forcing the edges of the hole closed. And don't hesitate. We get there and start right away. If I give the hand signal, we break and retreat back here." I looked around at the faces that alternated between staring at me and then at the ominous space hole. Signs of nerves abounded as I saw one of the greener girls having trouble standing still. A guy I knew as Mathew was twitching his jaw like he'd done a line of cocaine and I wondered to myself how the hell we'd be able to shut the larger ones if we couldn't get this one done. "This is not that big. It's not going to be difficult with the amount of Keepers we've got here," I added, trying to boost the morale a bit.

"It will be fine," Cormac said to me, but I knew the game. He was lying to me just as I had lied to them. We didn't know any such thing.

I hope so, I thought, but didn't say aloud.

He squeezed my hand, "Just don't get distracted. Keep focused."

"I think I could figure that out." I snapped, and knew I was on edge; perhaps overreacting due to stress.

"There's a lot of things I thought you'd figure out that you haven't."

I should've left it at that. I'd gotten nasty, he'd gotten nasty back. But I couldn't.

"You mean like figuring out that you used my friend to screw with me? Stuff like that?"

"Using her would have been sleeping with her. If I'd actually wanted her, I would have had her, and that's just stating the facts." He broke into a falsetto then "'I don't want you, no wait, I do want you' and then you hang all over Vitor. Maybe you had it coming?"

"So you used my friend? You thought that was the smart thing to do? No wonder we've got holes rotting away our universe, this whole operation is being run by an idiot!" It took me only a fraction of a second to regret what I'd just screamed in front of everyone.

Dodd cleared his throat and I realized we were already ringside to the massive space hole that was spilling radiation out and that we had raised our voices to the point that all the Keepers were avidly listening to our spat. "Not that this isn't entertaining," quite a few heads nodded as he said this, "But not enough to die from radiation poisoning for." They nodded for that too.

Maybe this was where I was meant to die, surrounded by a bunch of sarcastic assholes like myself, being killed by their leader because he looked like he was about to explode. Logic now entered my brain as my temper exited, screaming that he was an idiot in front of everyone was probably not on the top ten ways to handle things. Not that he wasn't and didn't deserve it, I just could've been slightly more tactful. I realized exactly how pissed he was when he switched places with Buzz so that he didn't even have to touch me as we began.

I took a deep breath, trying to shake it off. Time to get to work. A fight with Cormac wouldn't mean shit if I couldn't fix this.

I felt the tingle in my hands as the energy of all the Keepers started to flow through me and I concentrated every cell in my body to feeling the edges of where our existence ended and the strange universe started. Jagged and angry, it resisted the pressure. This felt so strange compared to a normal wormhole that just stretched open. Unlike a slit in a seam of clothing that can lie closed, this was a rip right in the center.

"I need more," I yelled down the line. I gripped Dodd and Buzz tighter as I felt more power flow from them. I closed my eyes, my sight was useless anyway. It wasn't working and it had to.

"More," I screamed. I could feel it in the way the energy coursed threw me, almost as jagged and unruly as the hole's edges; they were giving me every last ounce they had.

But it started to budge. Slowly, the edges started to creep closer together. I opened my eyes, wanting visual proof. It was slow, but it was working. Before our very eyes, we were altering the fabric of our very existence. It was awe inspiring. What else might we, as a group. be capable of?

It was half-closed now, and I noticed for the first time that the ground beneath my feet was spongy. I should've realized this earlier, we couldn't just stretch our world without something happening. The sand and earth that covered over the hole didn't just appear out of nowhere. We were stretching it and that would have repercussions. The electromagnetic force that keeps gravity from pulling us to the center of the Earth lost a little of its strength tonight. It was a small price to pay.

I measured the distance from where I stood now, to where the I had been before we started. I was closer to the center and farther from the cars. If the hole had still been the same size, I would've been standing a third of the way in it.

Almost finished, just a small gap was left when I felt a tingling near my ankle. Silver tendrils snacked around my leg. I looked over at everyone else but their concentration was firmly on the hole as it slowly closed.

I shook my leg and tried to knock it free but it clung with determination. It wrapped its way up my leg, like a boa constrictor, as I tried to not lose my concentration on the space hole. Only a few feet left and it would be closed.

As the edges finally touched, blocking out any sight of a foreign galaxy, I could feel the sides mesh together like there'd never been an opening. Laughter rose around me as we all shared in the same relief. We'd been fighting an uphill battle and this was the first time in a while I felt hope. We could fix this. We could fix all of this. We just needed to take out the senator before he could help anybody else get more wormholes up and running.

The silver coiled mist moved around my leg and reminded me of its presence. "Get off," I whispered to it. I didn't think it was going to do anything but then I felt a pinch. "*Get off,*" I whispered again, in a harsher tone. This time it dissipated into thin air.

It wasn't that I was ungrateful to it, whatever it was, but I had a group of Keepers here that I didn't want to freak out. I didn't think it would hurt me, but the fact it showed up out of nowhere was a bit unnerving. I thought it was tied to spells, like Vitor had explained. But there was no spell here, which meant there was something else at work that I didn't know about or understand.

I needed to stay calm and in control, and I needed to keep all the confidence of the Keepers, because I knew that the other space holes would be much harder. This one had already pushed them further than they'd ever gone already. I could sense it when we had all joined. There'd been a hesitancy at first.

Everyone was smiling and patting each other on the back. But when I looked at Cormac, I knew he was pissed. He was smiling at his people, but when his eyes landed on me they weren't smiling anymore. I got it. I didn't want to, but I undermined him in front of his people at a time we couldn't afford it. Considering all the shit he's done to me, I'd say we still weren't even.

"So where do we go now?" a couple of them asked, still riding high.

"New York?" another Keeper offered up.

"No," I said. "Now we kill a senator."

CHAPTER SIXTEEN

"I didn't expect a normal cemetery," I said to Vitor as we watched Hammond's body get lowered into the ground.

"We've got burial grounds on my planet that are similar to this."

As I looked around at the large crowd that had shown, I noticed the people certainly weren't of the normal variety as I spotted Fae and werewolves. It wasn't the largest turn out I'd ever seen but it was a healthy amount of a few hundred.

Cormac stood about fifty feet from me as he spoke to Burrom. I'd felt his eyes on me several times but every time I tried to catch him, he wasn't looking any longer. We hadn't spoken since we closed the hole the night before. When we'd returned to The Lacard, I had gone to my room and he'd gone to his.

"What's up with you two?" Vitor asked, noticing where my attention had been directed.

"It's nothing. He's just pissed off at me," I answered as I smoothed down my black dress.

"I wouldn't worry about it, considering."

"Considering what?"

"You know, the contract."

"The loyalty contract?"

"Strange name for it, but yes, that."

"What would you call it?"

"In your language? I'm not sure that it exists exactly. Maybe a prenup?"

If Vitor hadn't been so transfixed on all the different people coming and going, he might have noticed that I was about to lose my shit right then and there. It bought me time to calm myself down. I had to, and in a hurry. Vitor might have not noticed but Cormac had. He knew something was up and I didn't want this conversation interrupted.

I unclenched my fists and tossed my hair around as if I wasn't about to march over and kick the shit out of him. It worked; he went back to his conversation with Burrom and I was free to delve for more information.

"How do you guys use it? Is it the same as us?"

"We don't commonly use them anymore. Traditionally, they were used when we wanted to join two houses together but the children were too young to form an actual marriage. It was a place holder, of sorts."

"Did you ever break one?"

"I'm not sure about yours, but ours have varying time periods where if the relationship isn't consummated, the contract dissolves on its own."

I will not freak out and cause a scene at the

funeral. But oh, would he pay afterward. I didn't want to hear a thing about the idiot comment.

"Keepers can live forever so what's a few years if you change your mind?" Vitor continued.

"I still don't get how our brains stop us from aging."

"Yours do, ours don't."

"Why is that?"

"It's a Keeper thing. Even though Fae have a single consciousness, we don't know which genes are responsible for aging so we can't turn them off."

"Why didn't you guys work that into the deal with the original Keepers?"

"I wasn't around back then but everyone knows it was a non-negotiable. They were greedy buggers, your other half, that is. They were willing to let people in, but nothing else."

"You still have long lives."

"About three hundred years, which is a drop in the ocean compared to Keepers. On the other hand, you guys are dropping like flies so maybe you need them." We both looked at the casket after he said it. "You're down to less than a hundred now."

"And the information that was merged with our DNA is gone," I said sadly. If they could've just written something down, maybe we wouldn't be in this mess. "We're taking out the senator next...or trying to."

"I don't know if you can take the senator out."

"Maybe not, but we've got to try. Are you in?"

Complete silence.

"I'll take that as a no."

"I can't jeopardize my people."

"And what about the Earth?"

"We still have our planet."

I shook my head and walked away from him in disgust. As I stepped up to the casket and looked down at Hammond, I didn't feel mournful at all. If he had all of a sudden woken from a deep sleep, I might have tried to kill him myself. He was the major reason I was in this mess. He was around with the original Keepers when it was started and I found it hard to believe he hadn't had a hand in it. He brought this down upon all of us.

A group of twenty-two men and women, all arriving together, instantly drew my attention. They were led by a dark haired, lanky man, whose eyes darted from person to person, his body stiff.

"They're the defectors. The one in the lead is Linus," Cormac said as he came to stand next to me. He wore nothing but black from head to toe, except a glimmer of a gold watch at his wrist.

"We need to talk."

"I'm not ready to talk," he said mockingly.

The defectors were upon us before I could respond. They nodded in greeting. "We're here to pay our respects."

"Then do so and get out," Cormac replied in a tone closer to a growl.

"Thank you," I replied. "It's a nice gesture." Cormac bristled beside me as I said the words. He had a right to be upset with them but it didn't change a thing.

"I'd like to speak with you both," Linus said.

"Sure," I answered. Cormac didn't say no. We both looked at him and he still didn't seem to feel it necessary to speak. That was as good as it was going to get from him.

"We know what you did with the…" Linus paused.

"I like to call them space holes."

"We know you closed the smaller one. We've done some recon. We know how hard that must have been."

"And?" Cormac was not going to make this easy.

"We want to help you with the others."

"It changes nothing," Cormac told him.

"We aren't asking for that."

"Fine. Be in touch in two days from now."

Linus, and the few of his people that had hovered close enough to hear, walked away, back to the safety of the group.

We waited another hour or so before everyone left then we all drove back to The Lacard.

The streets were still empty, except for a few stragglers who carried duffle bags; they were clearly out looking for supplies before they went back to their hidey holes. Vegas was shut down, for all intents and purposes, like I'd never seen in my lifetime. It wouldn't be nearly as scary if I knew that I'd be able to kill the senator and put an end to this.

The Lacard, in contrast, was fully staffed today, not that it mattered. Nobody was out gambling anyway. I think as things got scarier, the staff thought this place was safer than most and were just looking for a reason to be here. Even before I actually knew anything about wormholes or aliens, wolves and Fae, there had always been this underlying current. It wasn't something you could explain to an outsider, we hadn't discussed it in the staff room, it was just a feeling that if the shit ever went down, this would be a bastion in the storm.

I looked at Cormac out of the corner of my eye as we climbed into the elevator with Dodd and Buzz. He was an angel and devil wrapped into one. The good was he'd keep everyone safe and together. The bad? He'd do it at any cost, even if he had to become the devil himself.

The doors slid open and Buzz and Dodd got out.

"I had to do it," Cormac said, as he beat me to the punch before we were even alone.

"How did you know?"

"Because it's very hard to hide something from someone as old as I am. I knew exactly what Vitor was telling you."

"You don't do something like that without telling someone," I started to scream.

"It's not forever. Would you have preferred to be stuck under Vitor's control? It was the only way to stop it."

"That doesn't make it right."

"I didn't lie. I just didn't explain the whole thing."

"How long does it last?"

"Five years."

"What!"

"Five years is nothing in our lifespan."

"Why five?"

"Because you would be twenty-eight by then and out of Vitor's reach. There was no other way."

"I want it broken like you said you would break all of them."

"So you can go stay with Vitor? No."

"Because I don't care what the Fae think of as legal age. I'm a grown adult and I'm sick of someone always trying to rule my world."

"If you want me to break it I will, but it won't end up being the only thing broken if Vitor thinks he's going to force the issue." His eyes were deadly when he said his next words. "Choose wisely."

The elevator doors opened to the penthouse floor and instead of walking to his apartment he made a left to the rooftop stairs.

"Don't walk away from me, I'm not done."

"I'm not. I'm going to the roof. You're welcome to come," he said as he continued on his way.

I watched the door to the stairway hang open and knew he was waiting for me.

I rounded the corner and he stood there. "I'm too tired to fight. This is my retreat. If that's what you are looking for, don't come. I promise I'll fight with you later, all you want."

It hit me suddenly, I'd never even realized that he might be the one mourning for Hammond. I'd barely known him but he had been a father figure of sorts to Cormac. I watched with fresh eyes as he climbed the stairs and walked toward the large weeping willow that sat by the edge of the roof. He sat on the bench underneath, just staring outward at the strip and the mountains beyond.

"I'm sorry," I said as I sat next to him. "I didn't realize what he meant to you."

He didn't speak and I didn't force him to. When

I would've left, he touched my shoulder, silently asking me to stay. I stayed until the sunset warmed the sky, neither of us saying a word.

CHAPTER SEVENTEEN

The details of the contract weren't as bad as I'd thought. It was really pretty cut and dry actually, as long as I didn't sleep with him, we wouldn't be married, beginning and end of it. Of course, I couldn't read the damn thing and he'd proven to be a little less than honest at times to meet his own ends, but I was going to accept it at face value. Partly because it was what I wanted to believe, and the other larger part was because I just couldn't handle another issue on top of what I already had going on.

The defected Keepers called in two days, as Cormac had told them to, and then two days after that. Problem was, we couldn't figure out a plan to get to the senator. He had nothing public scheduled for the indefinite future. As gruesome as it might sound, it needed to be a public execution. Odds were against us being able to take him down in the first attempt. If we could at least out him for what he was, it would drive him more into the open.

Secret Service wouldn't be protecting a monster. He'd lose his offices and security. His family was another question altogether. I personally wondered if they even were his family.

There I was, countless days after the first space hole appeared, weeks after the senator killed Rick, and we finally got a break. I sat, curled up on the couch, searching online and there it was; the senator had announced he'd be holding a televised appearance, around the corner from his office. He said in the press release that he was doing it to show his supporters that everything would be okay.

I wasn't buying it. There was an angle, I just didn't know what it was.

I dialed out but the call didn't go through. The cell service had become very sketchy; I wasn't sure if it was because they didn't have enough people to maintain the grid or if the space holes were messing with the signal. I grabbed the weird phone Cormac had given me yesterday. It wasn't as pretty as my iPhone, but I knew it would work.

Cormac's guys had erected a cell tower on top of the roof and on several other properties he owned. We now had the smallest cell service provider available but it was the most reliable. I knew what the implications were of what he was doing. It was for the same reason I had inventoried how much gas was in his private garage.

"Where are you?" I asked when he answered.

"Setting up more tower locations."

"We've got an opening."

"Conference room. I'll be right there."

I found Buzz and Dodd lounging in chairs

when I got there. I caught them up to speed quickly, since they'd only gotten a brief text from Cormac. He walked in just as I finished.

He sat down and didn't say anything right away. Finally, he leaned back and rubbed the dark shadow on his jaw. "We're missing something." He shook his head. "I think it's a trap."

"It doesn't matter. It's our only shot. The space holes have to be closed and we need him taken out first," I countered.

"Why? Can't we try to close them and then worry about the senator?" Buzz asked, unsure after Cormac shared his opinion.

"No," I replied. "I'm afraid to, especially after the smaller one. When that closed, I could feel the fabric of our existence thinning. If we close them all and he creates another tear afterward, I'm afraid it would be of a magnitude we could never heal."

"But the defectors aren't operating anymore."

"That we know of," Dodd added.

"Until we are positive we've got every other Keeper and the senator shut down, we don't attempt to close anything else," I said.

"There's something we aren't seeing," Cormac repeated.

"What do you guys want to do?" I asked Buzz and Dodd.

"We might not get another shot," Dodd said. "We just cover all the angles."

"I'm with Dodd and Jo. I think we go for it," Buzz said.

"Fine, it's your call," Cormac said looking at me. "We all sink or swim with your decision."

The senator had chosen the downtown mall outside the Golden Nugget underneath the neon lights to make his speech. I was shocked by the amount of people that had come out to see him, just to hear someone say everything would be okay. Countless monsters over many generations had come to power in this exact same way, but not this time, not this monster. Even if I didn't kill him, this would be the end of his career.

Cormac, Buzz and Dodd all had snipers aiming at the place he would take the stage. Even Dark was getting in the action and he posed as a blind man, perusing the perimeter for the unexpected, with Abby playing guide dog. I was playing decoy in the front row. Cormac hadn't liked the idea but it wouldn't have worked with anyone else.

When the senator stepped up, waving at a cheering crowd, he saw me and almost tripped; I knew it worked. He was completely disoriented and his eyes kept coming back to land on me.

"Ladies and gentlemen, I know that these are scary times and I promise to get the answers your government is withholding from you..." the senator opened to cheers from the crowd.

What a bunch of bullshit.

I looked at my watch. At exactly fifteen minutes in, they were going to simultaneously open fire. I'd agreed to this, but it wasn't my plan. They'd never have agreed to mine if I had told them. Cormac was right, I really did need practice at working as a team. I eyed the Secret Service, who were more relaxed now that everything seemed to be moving along smoothly, and I made my move.

I pulled out a Colt gun, jumped onto the stage and had the senator in a strangle hold with my gun against his temple in under ten seconds. The senator froze, bent over awkwardly since he was quite a bit taller than I. The Secret Service moved to rush me but stopped as bullets rained down around me and held them back, exactly as I hoped they would.

"This man is not who he appears to be," I screamed out into the crowd, as I waited for the senator to evaporate. Maybe he couldn't? Maybe when I touched him I interfered with his mojo somehow? Is that why I sensed he was afraid of me? I might never have this chance again. I pulled the trigger of my gun, jammed against his head, and watched the spray of blood explode everywhere.

He collapsed immediately. Before I could get another shot off, to make sure I'd killed whatever he was, someone, presumably the Secret Service, slammed me to the ground, ignoring the spray of bullets now. The gun was wrenched from my hand; I sent some juice to the guy holding me down but when he rolled off me, crying out in pain, another just simply took his place. I decided to wait this out until I could get a better idea of the numbers.

I'd be able to get away eventually, or Cormac would figure a way to break me out when he was done being pissed off that I'd gone solo. I'd thought it all through. I'd escape, lay low for about thirty years until they'd be looking for someone in her fifties and then be able to regain a normal life.

Immortality has some real perks to it.

The bullets had stopped and sirens blared in the distance as I was yanked roughly to my feet. I heard someone cry "He's dead!" in the distance as I was walked toward the waiting cop car. I also heard the words "Murderer!" being spewed at me and all I wanted to do was smile. He was dead.

It appeared that every last cop showing up for duty had swarmed in to help escort me to the police department. I was glad that I didn't have normal parents because this might have been a tad embarrassing for them. Me? I couldn't fit any other emotion in with the overwhelming relief that filled me.

The cop that held me read me my rights as I did the perp walk to the waiting squad car. My wrists were cuffed behind my back and there were about fifty other cops witnessing my departure. I didn't think I could take that many without having my hands free. I wished I had Cormac's melting metal ability. That trick would have come in handy right now. This cop didn't know how lucky he was.

The cop placed his hand on my head to duck me into the backseat when I heard shouts of pain and yelling. I jerked away from him and saw a man in a black ski mask, bent forward as he charged through the crowd like a linebacker. Every person he touched fell to the ground and cried out in pain.

A hand, presumably the cop behind me who was mad I had pulled out of his grasp, grabbed me by a fistful of hair and rammed my face into the car. I saw stars as another set of hands grabbed me, hoisted me up and carried me away from the scene.

I looked back through blurry eyes to see the cop lying on the ground in much worse shape than I.

"Take that, you big bully!" I screamed back at the cop on the ground.

The next moments flew by in a haze. A truck screeched to a stop so close that I thought it was trying to hit us. The back popped open and the masked man threw me in the back as he quickly followed me. We peeled out before the back door closed.

Cormac ripped off his ski mask and I saw Buzz in the front seat and Dodd behind the wheel. Dark and Abby were in the back.

"Can you ever go along with the program?"

"You know it had to go down like that," I said in my defense as I sat up.

"You should have discussed it with me," he screamed, but he had to in order to be heard over the sirens of the police cars chasing us.

"If the bullets didn't kill him, we needed everybody to see he wasn't human. They had to see him get shot like that, in their faces, with a lot of blood."

Dark leaned in on the conversation. "They definitely all saw it. The stage was a mess. It was gnarly, like a zombie movie come to life."

"And he was dead?" I asked, not caring about much else.

"He looked to be but that doesn't mean he'll stay that way. We still have no idea what he is, exactly."

I felt the stickiness on my skin and knew it was the senator's blood. I went to grab the towel and

Cormac stopped me.

"Hang on." He took a glass vial and scraped the edge along my skin, collecting a sample of the blood. "Now go ahead."

"What is this thing?" I asked referring to the truck that was stocked with all sorts of supplies.

"It's one of our emergency vehicles. I like to keep it stocked for occasions like this," Cormac answered.

"Have there been a lot of these occasions?"

"Not recently. I'm going to get this checked as soon as we get back." He packed the blood away.

The sirens started to fade and I looked through the back windows to see all the cop cars falling behind.

"This thing can move." We must have been cruising at somewhere near two hundred miles per hour.

"It's rigged for nitrous."

"Where are we going?"

"You wanted to close the space holes, didn't you?"

I nodded.

He placed a duffle bag, filled with clothes, next to me.

"Then we're heading to Mexico."

CHAPTER EIGHTEEN

We drove through the night to get to the space hole. The defectors didn't arrive for another seven hours, so we stopped at a resort on the coastline to rest up for the next day.

Cormac's Spanish was impeccable, or sounded like it. I wasn't sure what exactly he was saying but he seemed to be fluent.

"I got us a couple of suites," he explained as we left the desk with the keys. "This place should've been booked solid."

I looked around the lobby. Same as everywhere else: empty.

We ordered room service, fed Abby a couple of burgers and then we all crashed, exhausted from the day's events.

When I woke the next day, I found a pair of large sunglasses and a wide brimmed hat waiting beside the coffee.

"What's with this?"

"News of the senator's killing is on the news here," Cormac explained. "Just makes things simpler if you're not recognized."

"What are you doing?" I asked as I poured myself a cup of coffee from the room service tray. Cormac was piling seemingly random items on a table.

"Making some gold to bribe the Mexican government with so that they stay clear while we do our thing." He pointed toward four different piles. "Each metal type needs to be changed by itself."

"Can I do it?" I hadn't tried to do anything since I lost my nickel.

"Go ahead."

I grabbed a silver necklace from one of the piles and concentrated on thinking of gold. When I looked down at it again it was still silver.

"Why can't I do this?"

"Not every Keeper can do the same things. It just depends on what knowledge was embedded and passed on. Sometimes the genetic memory skips stuff. You might never be able to do it, but it doesn't matter."

It was still frustrating as I watched Cormac turn pile after pile of silver, then tin and all sorts of other metal objects, to gold.

"I'm worried about doing this hole with only the few of us and Linus and his men."

"It's not that much different in size to the Nevada hole. It'll be okay. We're better off having the other guys rest up before we try NY."

"Yeah, I know. Did you notice anything weird about the ground, after Nevada?"

"It was softer."

"Yeah." A knock at the door jarred my

attention, and I went to go answer it, Cormac hot on my heels. I turned and stopped before I got to the door.

"I can handle stuff on my own."

"Funny how you didn't complain when I was dragging you out of the swarm of cops."

"There's a difference, I needed some help then. Now I don't."

He stood back and with a flourish of his hand said have at it.

I opened the door to Linus, and his group who stood behind him, filling the hallway.

"It's for you," I said to Cormac. I hadn't had nearly enough coffee to deal with them yet.

"Don't look at her," I heard Cormac growl as I walked away.

Linus nodded. When it became obvious Cormac wasn't going to actually let them into the suite, I got dressed quickly and let Dodd, Buzz and Dark know we were leaving.

It took a caravan of SUVs to get us to the site. We stopped a good distance from the location of the space hole. Cormac and I drove in alone, with a suitcase of gold, to bribe the Mexican officials to play deaf, dumb and blind to our actions.

"What did they say?" I asked as two officials walked away with the suitcases.

"The gist of it was 'if you're stupid enough to get close to that thing, you'll be dead soon and not our problem.'"

"Oh well, that's nice."

We watched as they cleared the area. It wasn't as large as New York but it wasn't that much smaller, like we'd thought. Cormac let out a loud whistle and the rest of the SUVs came filing down.

The group piled out and we lined up just as everyone had in Nevada. It was a bit harder but didn't feel that much different. I could feel a bit more strength coming from this group. Maybe they had something to prove.

It was going exactly like the last time, except it felt perhaps a tad easier, until the silver ribbons started showing up.

I looked down at my ankles as everyone else stared, transfixed, at the massive space hole. The ribbons wrapped around my legs in an ever tightening vise. I tried to shake them off but all they did was start to nip at my skin.

Cormac looked at me, and then down at my leg.

"What the hell is going on?" he whispered.

"Ignore it," I told him and I tried to do the same.

I could tell he didn't like it but he didn't have much of a choice. The wormhole slowly edged shut and the ground around us softened. just like in the Nevada desert. The silver strands eventually gave up and disappeared again. The air felt slightly different, but I couldn't put my finger on what the difference actually was. Tingly didn't quite describe the charge that lingered.

Once we finished, we made arrangements to meet Linus and the other Alchemists at the marina in New Jersey two days later. From there, we would sail over to New York City and close the last and final hole and hopefully put this entire mess behind us.

CHAPTER NINETEEN

"What's going on?"

I collapsed on the bed in my room back at the suite. I'd hoped to be alone for a minute but Cormac had followed me in.

"I don't know what they are."

He grabbed my leg where the silver things had wrapped themselves around me.

"You're bruised," he said, as his thumb ran over the flesh of my ankle.

"Which won't last long."

He dropped my leg. "There is something off here. You can't tell me you don't feel it too."

"Of course, but what other choice is there?"

"I can't see another alternative, but I think the silver strands are trying to stop you."

"I know."

He turned and walked the length of my room. Cormac pacing was never a good sign. He finally paused and looked back to me.

"Every cell in my body is screaming out 'danger,' but I can't figure out another path to take."

"Because there isn't one. If we don't close the last hole in NY, who knows how unstable our universe will become. We might have had a choice at some point, but I don't remember ever having many options. It doesn't matter now because there is only one option left. We both know it." I crawled out of the bed even though I wanted nothing more than to crawl under the blankets and sleep for days. But we had to get on the road.

"What are you doing?"

"Taking a shower before we leave."

"Sleep for a while."

"I'll sleep in the truck on the way."

I watched as he shut the door to my room and slowly closed the distance to where I stood. He didn't say anything but he didn't need to. He didn't rush at me, but purposely took his time, and I realized he was making me silently acknowledge that I wanted him when I didn't move, just waited.

One arm curved around my back as his other cupped my neck, and his lips slowly sucked my lower one before he completely covered mine. And I wanted him, right then and there.

Then he pulled back.

"What are you doing?" I asked as he walked toward the door.

"Giving you time."

"Why?"

"Because there is no turning back, so you better be sure."

Then it hit me. "Because of the contract."

He paused by the door, his eyes intent, and he shook his head. "No, because of who I am. Once I get what I want, I don't let it go."

I was ready twenty minutes later and we headed out. The tension in the car was thick and somehow I managed not to be seated near Cormac for the majority of the ride back to The Lacard, where we'd take a plane to NJ. I needed to get my head clear for what was coming and he unnerved me.

I was reclined with my eyes closed in the front seat while Dodd took a turn driving, when the car suddenly swerving woke me.

"What the…" I didn't have to finish the question. A massive twister had just formed and touched down not even a mile from the car.

"Go left!" we all screamed at Dodd, and even Abby yelped, as the thing started to turn, looking like it would barrel down on us at any second.

He drove the Escalade off the road as we bounced all over the place, and watched the massive tornado grow larger and larger. We swerved around and got back on the road where we could drive faster. The four of us not driving turned in our seats, and Dodd watched from the rearview mirror, as the huge tornado tore up everything in its path.

"When did Nevada start getting tornados like that?" Buzz asked.

"Since Nevada started getting space holes," Cormac answered.

Nevada's had small twisters in her past, but the emphasis was on the word *small*. This thing was a monster, even by Tornado Alley standards. I'd never thought such a thing possible in the Nevada climate.

"The real question is, is closing them making things better or worse?" I knew Cormac was right about what he'd said. Something was changing. Buzz and Dodd knew it too. Their silence in answer to my question was deafening. We all felt it, but nobody knew what exactly was happening or what the hell we could do about it.

I leaned back in my seat and closed my eyes again, to block out the rest of the world and try to concentrate on another way to solve the problem posed by the space holes. Nothing, there was nothing.

"If we left the last one open, what then?" I asked aloud.

"Radiation would continue to spill out, with no end in sight. We would be okay but eventually it would spread to the point that a large chunk of North America would be uninhabitable. Eventually, over a long enough period of time, civilization would die, including us," Cormac answered. "I keep trying to figure out a way around this but I can't think of one."

"We have no choice," Buzz said. "We all know it. I'd rather die by fire than death by a thousand cuts."

"Agreed," I said. "It's got to be done."

I didn't realize the magnitude of what was wrong until we hit the Vegas Strip. It was empty, as it had been recently, but that wasn't what was surprising. What shocked me is it looked like a war zone. Several prominent buildings had crashed to the ground, street lights lay knocked over and there were several fires burning, grey smoke clouds hovering above.

The road became impassable about a mile away from The Lacard. Dodd stopped the car and we all got out.

Buzz and Dodd went to clear the road of several steel poles that were lying in the way.

"Just leave it. We'll get it later," Cormac told them as he started to walk ahead. He pulled out his phone and I heard Kever answer on the other side of the speaker. "What the hell happened?"

"Boss, it's real bad here. An earthquake of some sort hit."

"When?"

"About twelve hours ago," Kever responded.

We all did the math. Just as we we're closing the hole. I wanted to throw up. By the sounds coming from the bench Buzz just ducked near, he beat me to it.

"Why didn't you call me?"

"I tried. Cell service is completely down and you must have been out of range of the new circuit."

"Is everyone okay?"

"Yeah, there's a few more, though."

"What's that mean?"

"You'll see."

"I'll be there in a couple of minutes."

We walked the rest of the way to The Lacard at an uneven pace as we had to step over fallen poles and debris. It looked like a bomb had gone off and I hadn't even seen the worst. A large crack in the ground, ten feet wide, ran straight toward The Lacard Casino and then diverted around it, like a crazy weird moat. The Lacard stood there, in the mist of rubble, a pristine bastion, untouched. It was the only building I'd seen that appeared to have no damage whatsoever.

Buzz laid a large piece of fallen steel over the gap as a make shift bridge for us to cross. I found it humorous that Dodd carried Abby across. I felt a little woozy crossing it and grabbed on to Buzz's arm in front of me while Cormac followed behind. I couldn't see how far down the crack reached but I couldn't look for very long, without getting wobbly, either.

"Why didn't this crack run right up through the middle of the casino? Why is The Lacard untouched?" I asked.

Dodd answered from somewhere behind me. "Because the ground The Lacard stands on, and the ground surrounding the basement, is a fifty feet thick steel alloy of some sort. I don't know the exact mixture - it's something Cormac came up with. The building itself is made of some other type of metal he created."

"I can't believe it's still so perfect."

"Cormac always told me that this building would withstand anything."

I hung back a minute, still trying to get my bearings on what Vegas had become. Cormac walked in the main entrance with Buzz. Dodd, Dark and I entered a few minutes later and I was stunned to see a crowd of people all huddled in the main gaming room; there had to be at least five hundred of them. They weren't playing cards or games, they just sat, huddled in corners, some on the floor because of lack of chairs.

"Holy shit!" Dodd said next to me.

"They must have been forced from their hiding places when the earthquake hit." I scanned the room and saw evidence of cuts and bruises on many. Their clothes were torn and dirtied from the fallout.

When Dodd went still, I noticed him staring at something in the corner. It was Sabrina working on a cut on a little girl's arm. "She's a good woman. I wouldn't hang on the sidelines too long."

"You, of all people, should not be dispensing romantic advice."

"Fine. Suit yourself. In the meantime, what are we going to do with all these people?"

Kever walked through the crowd toward us and stopped by Cormac's side. "Why are these people huddled on the main floor?" Cormac asked.

"I didn't know what to do with them."

"Tell the staff to get them in rooms," he told him and then the two of them walked back toward us, out of the earshot of the crowd. Buzz walked over as well from where he'd been surveying the new guests in the corner.

"Any word outside of Vegas?" Cormac asked.

"No," Kever replied. "We haven't been able to get a line out. Everything is down. Cable, internet..."

"I know we said we weren't going to revisit this," I said, "but what happens when we close the space hole in NY?"

Everyone was speechless. There was only one way forward where civilization even had a chance of surviving. I looked again at the people in The Lacard, now being directed to different places by staff. Slow confirmed death or a chance at a future, but with pretty bad odds; I wondered which way they'd bet?

"NY it is. Let's just hope that maybe the damage is localized to where there used to be portals. We didn't see anything driving in, other than the tornado."

"Oh, yeah, you mean the F5? No biggie," Dodd said on the verge of hysteria.

I understood. The pressure was enough to make anyone crack.

"Kever, we're going to need everyone for this," Cormac instructed

"Even the Doc?"

"No," Dodd answered.

Cormac looked at Dodd for a moment and then turned back to Kever and shook his head. "She stays. Too many hurt people here. Tell everyone to be ready to leave for NY in five hours. Dodd and I are going to go get the 747."

He paused by my side before he left. "Rest." It might have been endearing if he had stopped there, but he didn't. "You're going to need it."

CHAPTER TWENTY

I lay on my bed in the penthouse and actually did try to rest, but I might as well have had coffee running through my veins, instead of blood, for all the good it did me. I tossed and turned until I heard a rap at my bedroom door that alerted me that it was time to go.

I threw on a pair of jeans and a shirt and grabbed the bag I'd packed in case we managed to live past tonight and I needed a change of clothes. We piled into the SUVs that would take us to the desert landing strip. We could've been headed to a funeral for all the enthusiasm I felt among the Keepers with me. How quickly things change. After the first space hole we had closed, we'd been walking on air. But, like so many things in life, we hadn't known all the details, and the full picture wasn't quite as pretty up close.

I'd thought killing the senator would be the hardest hurdle to cross. That turned out to have been a small stepping stone. Dodging the police was a nonissue. What police? I hadn't seen a single soul, other than the huddled masses on the casino floor, since the latest round of environmental disasters had begun. Those people certainly weren't in any position or desire to turn me in. They were clinging to survival; in life, that trumps pretty much every other want.

The large plane sat ahead of us on the paved strip in the middle of the deserted desert. It was quite nice, with the name Lacard painted across the side in gold lettering; probably the genuine thing. A plane this nice seemed like overkill to bring high rollers to a casino that was more of a front than anything else, but like everything to do with Cormac, nothing was ever what it seemed.

I climbed the stairs up inside and discovered the interior was even nicer. Leather lounge chairs and sofas were all around, with a bar in the corner of the large room. A gigantic flat screen was playing the news and I wondered how it was even getting a signal, since the entire area had gone dark.

I settled in closer to the TV to listen as the reporter spoke as we all settled in for takeoff.

"Someone change this?" one of the Keepers in the room with me yelled out, but I grabbed the remote before anyone could change it. I'd never been a news watcher but I would've beaten the guy to a pulp before I let him change the channel. I knew it was going to be bad but I had to know.

Picture after picture of destruction was being displayed on the screen. There'd been a tsunami in California that had devastated the coast and ten miles inland. Chicago looked worse than Vegas, with half of its skyscrapers now rubble on the ground. It wasn't just the U.S. either. They showed a picture of where the Eiffel Tower had stood, now a pile of scrap metal. Australia's Sydney Opera House was gone. And they were just buildings.

The reporter started to cry on screen when she said that no one had been able to get a human death count since what everyone was now calling the apocalypse had begun.

I heard the same Keeper who'd wanted to change the channel, Donald, laughing at something on the other side of the plane and I wanted to kick him in the teeth. The world was falling apart; there should be no laughter from anyone. I knew I needed to keep my anger in check. Donald, like so many others, was in denial. I knew that game. I'd tried it myself a couple of times. Just because I wasn't any good at it didn't mean I should deprive someone else of their relief from reality.

Cormac walked in and out of the main cabin several times during the flight and my feelings were as conflicted as ever. I wanted him in the most primal of ways but I wanted to kill him as well. I was still so angry about so many things. Having sex with him and then stabbing him to death just didn't seem like a good idea, and we're talking end of the world logic. If I couldn't rationalize it now, you know on a normal day it was seriously bad thinking.

I leaned back and spent the next hours of my life just watching what had become of Earth. What I'd helped make it.

We landed the giant plane in the middle of the

NJ turnpike, which was devoid of cars. In horror movies, they always show highways packed to the gills with abandoned cars, but this was different. When NYC had first been swallowed by the massive space hole, everyone had thought it was localized. Now they knew the disasters were everywhere. Where were they going to drive? There was nowhere to escape *to*. There was nothing left for anybody to do but board up their windows and sit by the door with a rifle, or a baseball bat for those that were a little late to the game and hadn't had time to stock up.

We made our way over to the same dock in Middletown, but this time, instead of a yacht, we took a small cruise ship. The defectors were on deck already. This was the largest group we'd had yet, at close to seventy, and I still wasn't sure if it would be enough. After watching the destruction on the news, I didn't want to admit it, but I was starting to hope it wasn't.

If I weren't capable of closing the hole, then I wouldn't be the cause of even more damage. The big problem with that was that the world would eventually die anyway. So there's the rub, did I cause more destruction and try to explain to human kind that I did it to save them, or did I pray I couldn't save the world and we all died together - but at least I wouldn't be the evil villain who ruined the Earth. Lucky for human kind, I didn't feel like I had a choice. I figured I would try to do what I knew was right, while I prayed I'd fail. Even if it meant I might go down in history as the woman who destroyed the world. There would be no historians left to repeat the tale anyway.

We sailed over the ocean until we dipped into the bay. Linus got his crew in line, along side ours, before we took the last jog to close the final gap and get us within striking distance of the hole.

Cormac took the place beside me. I was selfishly glad he was there. He took my hand in a firm grip, lending his support.

"I have to tell you something," I said to him.

"What's wrong?"

"I'm mad about a lot of things."

He didn't say anything, just waited for me to keep speaking.

"But if we die here, I want you to know... I don't hate you. I mean...you know."

He said nothing for a second and I thought he didn't understand at all. I was just about to open my mouth and take another bungled attempt when he smiled.

"I know. I don't hate you, too."

I nodded and looked down at the ocean waves, slightly embarrassed now.

"You ready?" he asked, bringing the dire situation back front and center.

Can you ever be ready to possibly destroy the Earth? I couldn't even get the words out. I was sure my face was tinged green from nausea at the thought of what might happen.

"Good," he said, in a normal tone, which I'm sure was for the sake of people listening on. Then he leaned in closer to me and whispered. "Just don't throw up because there's no way I'll be able to play that one off."

He raised his hand and I heard the engines roar as the boat started its slow churn forward. His fingers kept their grip on mine and I felt Dodd take my left hand, lending his own support. It was going to be a joint effort, but I'd be the lead as I was the strongest at this by far. Ultimately, the failure would rest on my shoulders.

We were within ten feet when I felt the silver strands start to wind up my legs. They were the last thing I needed.

I looked down at the strands weaving around my ankle. "I get it, you don't like this, but I'm doing it, so cut it out."

The god damn things pinched me then.

"I said, cut it out! It's happening and no amount of carrying on is stopping it. I don't have a choice."

"What are you doing?" Cormac asked.

I looked down at my ankles and the strands were gone.

"Nothing." I didn't have the energy to explain something unexplainable right then.

We dropped anchor at the edge of the abyss.

"On the count of three," I called out to everyone and began the countdown as we all linked together.

This was the biggest group of Keepers yet and the additional energy that was pouring into me almost made me feel high. I reveled in it for a selfish moment and then directed it toward the hole. Like the others, the edges rebelled against being closed. This hole was massive. I realized quickly I wasn't going to have enough juice.

Out of desperation, I had to go beyond just

directing the flow of energy and actively try to pull it from the other Keepers. I wasn't even sure how I was doing it but I felt it working.

In my peripheral vision, I saw many eyes looking toward me but nobody broke ranks as I forced them to offer up more than they had initially been willing to part with.

"Careful," I heard Cormac say. "Pull too much and you could kill them."

"Pull too little and we all die anyway," I replied.

"She makes a good point," Dodd chimed in on my other side.

I blocked them out as I used everything I had inside me to feel for the edges again and tried to force them to close. Just a little more. I just needed a touch more power and I knew I'd have it. I pulled on them and I felt the strain. I also felt the edges moving. Slowly, finally, the hole started to shrink.

The winds around us kicked up a notch, and whipped my hair into my face but I ignored it. I also pretended the boat wasn't rocking, dangerously close to capsizing, as the air started to howl. I felt the energy straining as Keepers became distracted but I pulled at them to make up for the difference.

Finally, after what had felt like hours, the edges of the tear in our universe touched. The city was gone for good; all its buildings and all the lost souls lost forever, but so was the space hole, filled in by ocean now. I released Cormac and Dodd's hands in our human link and collapsed on the deck of the boat in utter exhaustion. I heard a sigh of relief as everyone released each other's hands.

"How did you do that?" Dodd asked as he sank to the ground, looking as depleted as I did.

"Do what?"

"Force our energy from us? I swear, I don't think we could've let go if we had wanted to."

"We couldn't. I tried. That wasn't cool. You could've killed us," Linus said from his seated position against the other side of the boat.

"I didn't know I was doing it, but I would do it again." I cringed the minute I said the words, as I realized how much I had just sounded like Cormac in one of his overbearing moods.

"Something's wrong," Cormac said, the only one of us left on their feet as he paced the boat. Then he started to float and hover, clearly trying to get a better view of whatever he thought he was seeing. A bolt of lightning hit the water feet from us, as if in case anyone was doubting his instincts.

I gripped the side railing and dragged myself to my feet. I expected to see tornadoes in the distance, giant bolts of lightning and fires. It was all of those things and worse.

Chills ran over my skin and I couldn't find any words to describe the horrors in front of my eyes. I'd had happier nightmares. Besides the fires that were raging on the coastline, I could see creatures, for lack of a better word, walking the area. They weren't fully in existence, but they weren't *not,* either. They appeared, like ghosts, with a translucency to their features.

A large grayish one noticed us and glided toward our boat, skimming the ocean surface as it headed straight for us.

"What the hell is that?" a Keeper screamed.

"Start the engine, move this thing!" Dodd yelled.

"We couldn't outrun it anyway," Cormac said as he was standing next to me.

It closed the small gap and hovered over us a moment with a curious stare, sniffed the bow and then hissed before it moved away, not caring to be near us. The sky looked strange as well, with a shimmer that had nothing to do with stars.

"What the hell is going on?" Dodd asked.

I hadn't noticed him standing next to Cormac and I until he spoke.

"You know when you think you see something in the corner of your eye but you tell yourself it isn't real?"

"Yes."

"I think we just made it real."

"That is exactly what you did," a voice echoed in the air, everywhere and nowhere all at once.

We all circled and looked for the source. A cyclone of air started to blow and Keepers were thrown from the boat by the violent winds. Cormac, Dodd, everyone...thrust overboard several miles out to sea. The angry ghost like creatures moved out of their paths as they sailed through the air. At least whatever new form of creature they were, they had no interest in us.

The deck was clear except for me, I stood, without feeling even the smallest breeze, as the wind tunnel headed straight toward me.

I stood my ground and waited. It stopped five feet in front of me. The winds dropped off and a golden Adonis stood, looking at me from the same spot, blond hair flowing gently in the ocean breeze.

"Who are you?"

"Don't you recognize me?"

"What are you?" I asked him.

"You knew me as Senator Core," he said as he stood toe to toe with me.

"But *what* are you?"

He smiled. "I'm what the Keepers created. I'm the very core of our existence, of all existence, at the very smallest level."

"I don't understand."

"Of course you don't," he said as he laughed aloud in a giddy manner. He spun around with his arms outstretched to the sky as he took a deep breath. "Oh, to be alive and free," he yelled to the sky.

He turned back to me. "You don't know what it was like, being stuck in that human form."

"Why were you? I thought I killed you."

"You killed my host. The body I needed to live here, until now that is. You're not as stupid as I thought. The pieces are starting to fit together. I can see your mind working," he circled me now, examining me like a lab rat. "Every plane in the universe has its own requirements to exist. Your Keepers tried to destroy me but they couldn't. You can't destroy energy. The best they were able to do was rob me of my ability to exist on this plane. In essence, they maimed me. That is why I needed you to alter the physics of this universe in order to dwell here again. There are so many planes of existence, but you humans only see a fraction of what exists.

DONNA AUGUSTINE

Yes, you might unknowingly draw energy from the other planes, but you could never see what really existed all around you. The other planes weren't as strong, but once you thinned this world, that all changed."

"Why did you kill Rick and my foster parents?"

"That was payback. Your whore of a mother owed me a debt when I helped her barren form beget you." Then he started to cackle. "You're so obvious. You aren't of my flesh. I helped her get pregnant with Hammond's child, I didn't give her one of my own. She wasn't worthy. All she wanted was to get pregnant to give the wolves a Keeper they could control."

"Why would you help her?"

"It was the deal. She helped me escape the prison the Keepers had put me in by bringing me a body. The Keepers had stolen the one they had given me."

"Did you kill her?"

"No, the wolves did that when, in the end, she refused to hand you over to them. A sudden attack of guilt, I guess. Pathetic humans." His voice was filled with contempt.

"Which wolves killed her?"

"I don't know which ones did it, nor do I care. They were just a pack of mongrels to me."

"Did you ever want to help them?"

"Those filthy things? Talentless and stupid, I liked them less than even you. But I needed to get your bleeding heart father on board and some of the other Keepers."

"It was about this, the whole time. Creating

tears that would then alter the universe."

He had a hard time keeping his attention focused; I got the sense that he was a bit enthralled by his own form, the way a little girl would twirl in a new dress, as he constantly shifted about the deck. "It's why your father killed himself. I wasn't sure you would be able to repair them on your own. He had figured it out. After you, he was the second most adept at altering the fabric of the planes of existence."

"Why are you telling me all this?"

"Because it no longer matters. There is no turning back," he replied as he walked around the deck. "You've merged the planes of our existence. You've melded this world with the place magic lives."

I looked around again and knew he was right. Everything felt slightly different, looked different, more intense. The air felt the way it did when lightning was about to strike and everything had a crackle to it.

"It's time for us to say goodbye now," he said. "I can't have you lingering around in my world. You're now a liability."

He turned and smiled again and I knew he was going to try to kill me. I didn't blame him, I had the same intention toward him.

I thought he was going to come at me, but he didn't. He raised his hand and directed a dark tendril of smoke toward me. I watched it gather and realized the resemblance it had to the silver ribbons that had been appearing around me. Strand after strand gathered in his outstretched hands until with a quick burst of motion, he released them on me.

I tried to dodge them but they were like heat seeking missiles and they followed me down onto the deck.

They started to burn my skin, but that wasn't the worst part; they started to bore into me. I tried to get to my knees, if I could just get a hold of the senator, maybe I could take him out, but I couldn't even get to my feet.

"You thought you had a chance of killing me?" he said as he towered over my crippled form. "I helped create you! You were nothing but a means to an end. If I hadn't needed you I would have helped the wolves rip your mother and you to pieces."

I was dying. I knew it. I would leave this world in a shambles with this monster at the helm. A slow death would have been preferable. At least they would've had a few good years. Now they had nothing but terror.

And then they came. My silver ribbons of smoke. They wove around me, cocooning me.

"What are you doing?"

I looked toward the senator, who looked furious.

"How are you controlling those?"

"The same way you are controlling that black smoke."

"You idiot. You have no idea," he replied. He poured a little more of the black smoke my way but it didn't matter, my silver ribbons dissolved anything that came at me, quickly and seemingly effortlessly.

Then they went on the offense. Strand after

strand gathered and started to nip away at him, at the flesh of his form.

"Get off me!" he screamed.

"No," I said as I got to my feet. I was bloody and in pain but I didn't care, I would see the end of him.

"I command you to get off," he screamed but they didn't listen.

He let out a howl that filled the air; I imagined it could be heard for miles. The air kicked up into a vicious storm and I saw the tornado start to form around him.

"Oh no…" I leapt in his direction but all I got was air. He was gone.

The moment he left, I hung over the edge of the boat and tried to locate Cormac, Dodd and the rest of the Keepers, who were all swimming back to the boat from pretty substantial distances.

One by one, as they reached the boat, they floated up and onto the deck, Cormac in the lead.

"Are you okay?" he asked, gripping my arms and looking at my torn clothes and the gashes that were already healing. He didn't wait for my answer but started checking me for mortal wounds.

By time his gaze met mine, I could see the intensity there.

"I thought you were going to be die," he said.

"I almost did," I replied in a joking way, more from nerves and the thrill of having survived.

His arm wrapped around my back, pulling me snug against him and then his mouth was pressing on mine. It was nothing like the gentle invasion of his last kiss; a raw hunger that made my limbs feel weak took over.

His mouth left mine but he still held me close as he whispered in my ear, "You know how I gave you a choice before we came here?"

I knew exactly what he was talking about and nodded my head.

"I'm taking it back." He released me to watch his men come aboard and join us.

I laughed at his joke but he didn't.

"Cormac? You're kidding, right?"

He gazed down into my eyes without a hint of a smile and then said, "No."

He turned toward the rest of the Keepers that had made it back on deck, while I stood trying to get my bearings.

"We saw a silver haze envelope the whole back of the boat," Dodd said. "What happened?"

I gave all the Keepers a rundown of the events after they'd been thrown from the ship.

"So all this.." Buzz waved his arm around to encompass the strange creatures that were flying around, "the storms and weird weather? All here to stay?"

I collapsed on the bench, took another look around and turned back to the Keepers, who were now looking to me for an answer.

"Welcome to our new universe."

THE END

More in The Alchemy Series coming soon!

Sign up here to be notified of new releases by Donna Augustine, including the continuation of The Alchemy Series.

Visit us on the web at www.DonnaAugustine.com

Made in the USA
Lexington, KY
02 December 2013